Homo

Homo

Michael Harris

James Lorimer & Company Ltd., Publishers
Toronto

For Nicholas

James Lorimer & Company Ltd., Publishers acknowledges the support of the Ontario Arts Council. We acknowledge the financial support of the Government of Canada through the Canada Book Fund for
our publishing activities. We acknowledge the support of the Canada
Council for the Arts which last year invested $24.3 million in writing
and publishing throughout Canada. We acknowledge the Government
of Ontario through the Ontario Media Development Corporation's
Ontario Book Initiative.

Cover image: iStock

Library and Archives Canada Cataloguing in Publication

Harris, Michael, 1980-
  Homo / Michael Harris.

(SideStreets)
Issued also in an electronic format.
ISBN 978-1-4594-0192-1 (bound).--ISBN 978-1-4594-0191-4
(pbk.)

  I. Title. II. Series: SideStreets

PS8615.A74793H66 2012   jC813'.6   C2012-903699-4

James Lorimer & Company Ltd.,   Distributed in the United States by:
Publishers   Orca Book Publishers
317 Adelaide Street West, Suite 1002   P.O. Box 468
Toronto, ON, Canada   Custer, WA USA
M5V 1P9   98240-0468
www.lorimer.ca

Printed and bound in Canada
Manufactured by Friesens Corporation in Altona, Manitoba, Canada in
August 2012.
Job #77088

Chapter 1

"You're going to burn that marshmallow."

"Shows what you know. The burned bit's the best part." Julie pulled her flaming stick out of the fire and waved it around, throwing off sparks and smoke.

"Watch it," snapped the girl next to us. She swatted ash off her sunburned shoulder and pushed herself off the log. "What a princess," smirked Julie, glad to be rid of her. The girl wandered away into the night in search of saner company. Julie tugged at the black skin of her marshmallow, revealing a second, gooier option beneath. She popped the burnt coating in her mouth and kicked back, shutting her eyes in pleasure.

I smiled at her in the dark and gave her a nuzzle with my shoulder. There were maybe fifty of us up there at Cultus Lake for the end-of-summer party. Some drunk guy called Nicholas had already fallen into the bonfire. His friends had had to cart him away in the back of a pickup. He was howling like an animal and clutching where his charred T-shirt had fused to the bloody skin underneath.

Everyone was drunk and wandering, or huddled together and speaking excitedly about things they'd never remember in the morning. Someone on the other side of the fire, invisible in the flickering light, kept saying, "I don't know. I just don't know."

Julie tossed a pebble through the flames to the feet of the mystery man. She shouted, "What? What don't you know?"

There was a pause, then the sloshing sound of a bottle and the voice again: "I don't know." Whoever it was stood up and stumbled away. We never did find out who it was.

Some time passed. Julie and I just leaned against each other and fed broken things to the fire. We listened absently to kids stumbling down to the black lake. We saw them stumbling back up again, wide-eyed in their sopping underwear and stealing glimpses of each other's bodies. Wet fabric made every bulge blatant.

Julie and I were holding a whispered conference about the start of grade twelve, about the big, blank future that stretched on after school. We passed a Thermos full of OJ and vodka back and forth. By the time we neared the bottom, I'd realized my only plan in the world was to get out of Chilliwack. I touched Julie's knee and told her, "I don't think I'm ever coming back, you know."

"Back from where?"

"University. I'm going to Vancouver to get my degree and that'll be that. I can't come back here. So I'm afraid you'll be forced to come with me, yeah?"

"To Vancouver?"

"Oh, Julie. Julie-baby . . ." I kissed her on the cheek and wobbled her knee too roughly with my hand. "We could have such an amazing life out in the city. I'll get a job and you'll get a job and we'll live in some broke-down house with a big dopey dog. We never need to come back here." As if to underline my statement, someone tramped out of the bushes behind us and began vomiting.

"Sounds nice," she said, but sadly. "You know I can't leave my grandma, though. Not with Dad the way he is. You know that." Julie looked up at the black cedar branches and continued. "He gets drunk all the time now. It's just getting worse. If I wasn't here, nobody would even change my Lola's shit bag."

"Oh, come on."

Julie ignored me. "He'd end up putting her in some gross care home, and she'd give up in a place like that . . ." She shook her head and put on a smile to spirit all that away. "But Vancouver sounds amazing. One day." And she leaned in to kiss me. Not our usual cheek-kiss, either, but a full-on mouth deal. I could smell the sour booze on her breath. The touch of her lips on mine snapped me awake.

"Whoa. Whoa!" I had her by the shoulders and

was smiling at her with concern.

"It's okay," she said. "It's okay." And she tried to go in to kiss me again.

"Not okay," I straightened my elbows and shuffled down the log. And then it came out, slipped out like an apology. "Julie, you know . . . you know I'm gay."

She sighed and sort of dropped into herself an inch. "I guess I knew that." She drained the Thermos and wiped her mouth on the sleeve of her hoodie. "Good on you for finally saying it, though."

Silence. Fire crackles. "I figured it was obvious by now."

"I guess it was . . ." She was nodding her head and digging at the fire with her marshmallow stick, letting the goop on it get coated in ash. "This is better, by the way. A better rejection, I mean, than the one in grade eight."

"Anything is better than what I did in grade eight."

"Oh, lots of people dump their girlfriends by text message."

"Do they?"

"It was the sad-face emoticon that pushed it over the edge."

I took the Thermos from her and tucked it into the backpack at our feet. "You're the first one who knows," I told her. "Other than my parents, I mean."

"You told your *parents* before you told *me*?"

"Well, technically it was a porn site that I'd left on my computer that told them."

"Oh." She looked dreamily around at the camp-site. "I'm going to bed, okay? Try not to wake me later?" I watched her burrow into our tiny blue tent and pass out fully clothed on the rollout mattress. I went over and tugged my army blanket over her and zipped the door shut. Then I took myself for a last walk down to the lake. It was late — so late the tawny edges of morning were already bruising the sky. The birds argued in the trees.

I was alone at the water's edge. I took out my phone for comfort — the way I always do when I don't want to think. I pulled up a mapping app and told my phone to find me. And there was the little blue dot, hovering above a lake in the middle of a mountainside. Nearby were some chicken-scratch lines making up the few streets of Chilliwack.

I pinched my fingers on the screen and stretched them out to make the map zoom out — then again, again — until I was so far above things I could see the outline of British Columbia. I zoomed down again, letting myself land in Vancouver this time, a great big mass of lines with street names I didn't recognize. It was an hour's fast drive away, but might as well have been another world.

I stayed by the lake for a while, waiting for something to happen. But when nothing — nobody — came, my head started to nod. I hiked back up to the tent. Inside, I curled in a big-spoon position next to Julie. She mumbled something too quiet to hear, and I said, "Love you, too."

Chapter 2

Julie had promised to meet me out front before the first day of school, but she was nowhere to be seen. A crush of kids was milling around on the lawn in front of Spencer High. I was slowly turning in the middle of the crowd, trying to look like I wasn't missing anyone.

Then, there she was, grinning like crazy and daring me not to notice she'd shaved off all her blue-black hair. "Look at you. Look at you," I mumbled. And I stretched my arms around her. "So what's this?" I finally laughed, running my hand over her stubble.

She gave me one of her looks. "Dad decided to give me a haircut after a few beers. By the time he was done, this seemed like the best option."

"Well, you look amazing."

"Tell that to my dad. He wasn't so hot on the 'lesbian look.' His words. Actually, I think he mainly thought I was insulting his barber skills."

"Which you were."

Julie shrugged and looked around at the packs of dogs that were our schoolmates. Their mouths were barking, they were crashing into each other, they were even fighting over scraps of food. It was enough to make you sick. But Julie Matining always kept a certain distance from the pack anyway. She was Filipino for starters, the only one in our very white school. She was also killer smart — even if she knew how to cover it up.

I thought we'd go in together. But Julie caught sight of the kid who'd fallen in the fire up at Cultus Lake the week before. She wanted to go over and check on him. "By the way," she said, already half-gone, "I know you're not on Facebook, so you might wanna know that you being gay is sort of all over it."

"Julie . . ."

"It wasn't *me*." She waved around at the crowd. "It was just, you know, the *Internet*."

"That doesn't even —" She was gone already. She joined the semi-circle of girls around Nicholas and was reaching to touch the scars on his chest while he held up the front of his T-shirt.

The first bell rang and everyone swarmed the main door to get to class. I hung back on the front lawn and waited for the crowd to pass me by. A hand slapped the back of my head, hard. A voice said, "Get a move on, faggot," in a breezy, matter-of-fact way. But there were so many kids, I couldn't tell who had done it.

I was alone on the lawn. For a minute I just looked at the concrete building and thought about leaving. I thought about walking down to the Cottonwood Mall and spending the day reading magazines at the shitty café they've got there. What horrible thing would happen if I didn't go in? I could toss my cellphone in a garbage can and let tomorrow take care of itself. In fact, I was wobbling on my heels, almost gone, when Julie came rushing back out with her head down, working her phone.

My own phone started vibrating angrily in my pocket. I read a text from Julie (*Where u at?*) just in time for the real Julie to start badgering me. "C'mon! What are you doing?"

Good question. I gave her puppy dog eyes as a joke and then realized I meant it. Suddenly, I was a weak little kid. "Maybe I'll just —"

But she grabbed my arm and started speed-walking me toward the door. "You know that university degree you were telling me about?" she said. "You remember that life in Vancouver? They don't give out student loans unless you're actually a student."

So I switched over to automatic, and we heaved ourselves through the entrance. Because . . . because that's what you do. The bell rings and you go where you're supposed to. Principal Weightman was patrolling the hall. He saw us shuffling along and barked, "Well, we're off to a fine start, aren't

12

we?" Really sarcastic. Julie ignored him and I mumbled an apology. We kept walking down that empty hall.

Julie was talking about her electives, but I was thinking about all the tiny lives people were about to lock up in those tiny lockers. People, most people, don't have much to show for their lives, I figure. Most people, if you bust open their locker, will disappoint you with how boring the contents are. Gym clothes. A mouldy sandwich. Maybe, if you're lucky, a badly written love letter shoved between pages of homework.

"Hello? Hellooo? Earth to Will." Julie smacked me on the cheek — first with a gentle hand and then her lips. She'd delivered me to my home-room. "You're on your own till lunch, bucko." She thumbed the lipstick off my cheek. "Try not to get stuck in a corner or something."

I sat in my classes, in the rows on rows of gaping kids, all whispering about some YouTube video I hadn't seen yet. I got counted by teachers. *Will Johnson? Present. (Tardy.)*

They must have talked about something, those teachers, but I was too busy eyeing the crowd to notice. It's important to really look around you on the first day, you know? Get the lay of the land.

First: there was a disturbing lack of hot guys at Spencer High. I made do with Adam Becker — a guy with a workable mix of hockey muscles and Sunday-school hygiene. Big shoulders, hair slicked to one side in the finest Mennonite fashion, and a tendency to wear tight pants. He wasn't someone you could really talk to, but you could stare at him if you sat in the back row. While Adam drew dirty pictures in his physics notebook, I sketched the buzzed back of his head. Pathetic.

Daniel Federline sat in the back row of physics, too. He was definitely there for the Becker view. Before my Facebook exposé, Daniel was the only gay guy in our grade. I know they've got queer clubs in city high schools. But when you live in tiny Chilliwack, an hour's drive from anywhere, you don't have the luxury of what they call a community. You've got Daniel and me in the back row, pretending not to be pervs. We orbited the rest of the students like a pair of asteroids.

But Daniel was never any good at hiding his staring, especially when it came to guys like Adam Becker. Daniel sat with his legs crossed lady-style and just drooled over Adam. "I'm a muscle queen," he whispered to me, leaning across the aisle. He gestured at Adam's back and asked, "How about you?"

I tried to ignore Daniel, but he kept on staring with his head cocked to one side. Before long, Adam's girlfriend, Laura Kwan, had turned around and caught Daniel staring. While the teacher went on about "expectations of the course," Laura leaned back and pointed her pen at Daniel. "Get your own boyfriend, homo."

Daniel gave me an eye roll and I focused on not knowing him. He'd been pushed around a lot since junior high. Into lockers, through doorways — even, once, down the stairs. His mistake was being obvious, that's what the other guys kept saying. "Why do you have to be so *obvious*, Daniel?"

I guess what they meant was *Why do you have to be gay for real?* Which is why my first "for real" day at school was already freaking me out. Chilliwack is more of a church-town than anywhere in the country. So I was *awake*. In towns like mine, you keep your guard up.

Mr. Hix started droning about the grade system. I stared at this poster he'd stuck up on the wall behind his desk. It had a bunch of kids of different races all laughing in a meadow with the word *"Tolerance!"* blazing over their heads. Freaky. You *tolerate* a teacher's bad breath. You *tolerate* your mom's annoying friends. And, on that first day of grade twelve, I got the feeling that a lot of the kids, and even the teachers, were *tolerating* me.

At lunch I walked by Adam in the hall. He and his overgrown friends were laughing about a movie they'd all gone to. One of them was saying, over and over again, "That was so gay, man. Omigod, it was *so* gay." Then I guess they spotted me. I guess my face got red.

"I don't mean it like *that*, Will," the one guy started. "Don't get all delicate now. We've already got Daniel Federline for that."

I really didn't feel like stopping to talk this one out. So I mumbled, "I know, I know, it's cool," and kept going. I saw Adam give me this look, though — a warning sneer with half-bared teeth. In a flash I wondered if he knew I'd been looking at him in class. Maybe he could feel me staring at his back, or maybe someone had warned him about the perv two rows behind him. And I thought to myself, *So, this is the beginning of looks like that. Looks that say, "Don't worry, I tolerate you."* I wondered if Adam's church was the tolerance kind or the eternal hellfire kind. Or maybe, worst of all, it was both.

My ears were getting hot so I walked faster down the hall. Julie would be waiting to eat lunch with me at our usual spot in the teacher's parking lot, where nobody else ever went. But I needed to get somewhere on my own first. I ducked into the handicap washroom, the only place in school where you can lock the door against the world. I scowled at my red ears in the mirror and told the reflection, "Don't get all delicate now."

If you find yourself locked in handicap washrooms as often as I do, you know there's not much to do in there. That's what I like about it. You figure out the pattern in the tiles, you read the horny graffiti. Maybe you splash your face. But then there's just . . . space. For once in the big, noisy world, nothing's coming at you.

Before I left, I looked at the guy in the mirror again. I wondered if I would think he was cute — if he sat down next to me, say, and asked what I was reading. A little short, but not weirdly so. A too-small chest under an old flannel shirt. A mess of brown hair and muddy brown eyes. A lopsided grin. If there had been a grin. Cute, I guess, though sort of stunned looking.

I decided that, yes, I would think the boy in the mirror was cute. My skin had finally cleared up that summer, so I'd stopped avoiding my reflection. I'd even stopped brushing my teeth with the lights off. That was something.

When I cracked open the door, I could still hear Adam and his buddies howling down the hall. They were on to something else — seeing how far they could spit. I wondered whether Adam was thinking about me at all.

Nobody knows what other people are thinking. We all live in our own movies, our own dramas. So maybe Adam really did sneer at me, but maybe he just wasn't in my movie. Maybe, in his movie, his life, his dad was dying of cancer, or his cat got murdered by raccoons. Or maybe that's just what Adam's stupid face looks like when he isn't thinking of anything at all.

***

After the three-o'-clock bell, I sat and drew perfect little cubes in my notebook until it was safe to leave. Once the halls were clear, I made my way past a couple of janitors arguing about the best way to tape a piece of cardboard over a window some kid had smashed.

"This place is a death trap," said one of them. He poked at a patch where black mould was eating the ceiling. I decided to take the guy at his word.

I got outside just in time to watch the last bus pull away, taking a couple dozen screaming kids to their snug, stuccoed homes. One guy leaned out his window and gave me the finger. At first I thought he did it because he'd heard about me being gay. And then I decided he was just an animal and would have fingered anybody dumb enough to be standing alone on the sidewalk while the last bus leaves. He was wearing a broad, sloppy smile, like giving someone the finger was the wittiest thing he'd thought of in a long time. I watched that boy fade into the distance, thinking, *Go on. Tell me what you really think.*

Once the bus had turned the corner, I let out a sigh I hadn't realized I was holding in. I tugged the straps on my backpack and started home. It wasn't too far. Besides, it felt right to be walking on my own.

Chapter 3

That night, Mom and Dad were being weird. More weird than usual.

I was trying to read in the family room, but Dad turned on this reality TV show about fat people who confront their skinny families. In one segment, the fat sister made her mom and dad watch her eat, like, a gallon of ice cream. She kept saying, between drippy spoonfuls, "This is who I am, okay? This is who I *am*!" Dad thought this was just about the best TV he'd ever seen. He was sitting in his leather lounge chair, still wearing his grey realtor suit, and he was tearing up. He kept taking off his glasses to rub his eyes. Then he'd look over at me and say, "Can you believe this? Can you believe how brave that girl is?"

"Hm?" I looked up from my magazine and watched the fat girl cry for a bit. "Don't you get bored of these shows?" I asked him.

Dad blinked at me. "No."

I waved at the TV. "I mean it's not like these are real emotions you're having. It's just a sugar-high for your brain. Like, when I came out to you and Mom, you didn't cry. You didn't anything. You just sort of stared at me." I shut up pretty quick then, because I could see his face starting to freeze up.

He kept his eyes on the TV as he said, "You know, Will, you didn't actually *come out* to us. We had to drag it out of you."

Neither of us said anything after that. We watched the next show, where a heroin addict got through five months of rehab. Dad started to turn away and wipe at his eyes again. When the show was over, he got up to go to the bathroom. Turning at the door, he said, "Well . . . well, you know we still love you and all that." Which was the closest he'd ever come to saying he loved me in the first place.

Dad's a good guy, by conventional standards. He's way better than Julie's drunken father, who has been wandering around their basement like a troll ever since Julie's mom died. If Dad had a straight son, he would know what to do — smirk about girls, clap in the sidelines, perform all those easy things that say "Yes, we're in this together."

When he was young, he was the good-looking kid in school who was nice to the nerds. I know this because my mom was one of the nerds. She tells this story of how her heart would shake when

Brady Johnson talked to her in the cafeteria. ("I'd be sitting there with my friends and we used to cry about how nobody would ever want to marry us. We were too tall or too stupid or too ugly. And your father just walked over from the cool kids' table and asked if I liked my sandwich. I mean, he just didn't care at all that I still had braces.") A real civil-rights champion, my dad.

Now, at forty-five, he was sort of worn down by spending the last twenty years selling houses in the valley. On the bus shelter by the mall there was an ad with his face on it. *"Brady Johnson doesn't just sell houses. He sells dreams!"*

I guess Dad used to hitchhike through Europe, and build homes out of mud bricks for poor Mexicans. But, like most people over forty, somewhere along the way he got tired. Now he just wanted to watch his shows. His favourite way of falling asleep was in that chair, the remote control clutched in his hand.

I heard Mom calling me to dinner. On the TV, a weeping father was saying, "We accept you, we love you for who you are." I pointed the remote control but waited until he was done blubbering before I switched him off. Then I wandered into the kitchen to face Mom.

She was being weird in a different way from Dad's weird. Dad's weird was easier to handle. With Mom, you really had to be *on*. Because, man, she was shooting her weird *right at you*.

As I set the table, Mom beamed at me with her

21

super-friendly nervous eyes. "Hey! We're going to get to your first day at school, I promise, Will. I want the scoop. But I just have to tell you guys first about what happened at pottery club. You're going to bust something when you hear this. I mean, I went into the pottery place — you know, down on Summerset. And, boys, I looked around and it was *full* of hippies. I mean, these girls were wearing their hair up in the funniest ways, all tied with pieces of twine, and I don't think one of them had a bra on. I think most of them drove in from the interior, because I definitely did not recognize them from around here. Like, I mean, these were lesbians — pretty much for sure. And I just thought, I just thought . . ." She plopped a lasagna down in the middle of the table to emphasize her next point. "I thought *How cool is this?*"

I should explain about the clubs. The more time Dad spent in front of the TV, the more Mom busied herself with groups. Part of me felt responsible for my parents having to distract themselves like this. I couldn't remember them being so out of it before I came out, so there had to be a connection. But, then, maybe I was only noticing how distracted we all already were.

No, I decided, Mom was definitely getting worse. She had joined a knitting club, a women's book club, a yoga club. Even an "appetizer club" where four women made big batches of appetizers and shared them with each other. For real.

I opened the freezer to get ice for my water and

stared at 400 tiny pastry things covered in frost fur. "Your appetizer club is going to make us all fat," I said.

"I'm a joiner," she said. "Some people are loners. I'm a joiner."

"All those clubs would make me crazy," I told her as I collapsed into my seat. "It's like you actually look for extra ways to feel obliged. Like you can't fill up your own time." Even as I said it, I knew I'd done some damage. Sometimes I'm like a toddler with a gun. I didn't know I'd hurt her until I saw that look in her eyes.

"It's good to be part of something, Will," she said, her face flushed.

She started methodically slicing the lasagna. "Being part of something is *healthy*," she said to the knife. "But you never did like playing in groups when you were little." This was her way of getting back at me — she could tell me about myself as a child. "You would always just go off and read a book on your own."

And that sort of freaked me out. If I wasn't like Mom, if I wasn't a joiner, then I would have to be a loner like Dad. I would end up drifting into a black hole from the comfort of some worn-down couch.

So that night, I sat at the dinner table and sized up the two of them, my two options for the future. I guess they didn't notice, because they were chatty and started asking me questions about school — was everybody nice and did I like my teachers and all that crap.

Mom got sort of intense when we were finished our lasagna. "And everybody was . . . nice, you said? No teasing?"

She was worried I'd get beaten up for being gay.

"Mom, it's not the 1980s," I said. And that sort of shut her up. She smiled tightly down at her hands and made to start collecting our dishes. I stood and took them from her before she got far. "Sit down," I said. "I can do these." It was a trick Mom and I kept playing on each other. Whoever did the dishes was actually escaping the table, while the other had to sit and talk to Dad. She handed over her stack of plates and smiled warily as she shifted back down into her seat.

Later, Dad and I watched more reality TV and then I went up to bed. It's my favourite part of the day, leaving the world.

But that night the words in my magazine wouldn't grab me. I surrendered to a kind of un-thinking trance. I just lay in bed, half-dressed and stared at the ceiling. There were funny little cracks in the plaster, and it sort of calmed me down try-ing to find pictures up there — like plotting out new constellations.

Sleep wouldn't come. I sat up with my back against the wall and stared at my laptop. It was sleeping and my screen saver was a slow grey cloud that swirled around, turning black, then grey, then black again. Really trippy. It made me think about a story I'd read that summer in one of my magazines.

It was a story about dark matter. From what I

could understand, it's the stuff in space that no-body can see. They only know it's there because of the pull it has on everything around it. The thing that really got me was that *most* of the universe is dark matter. That made my head feel sort of quiet. I sat on my bed and thought how awful it was that you can't even *look* at most of the universe. Even if we learn how to travel at the speed of light, our puny eyeballs won't show us what we discover. I guess the black clouds of my screen saver were my idea of what dark matter would look like, if it ever showed its face.

I thought about the Internet, and the trillions of websites and blogs and porn videos just flying through the air and through everybody's brain. I thought if I knew what to type into a search en-gine, maybe I could be chatting with some really great guy in no time.

But I didn't feel like it. Not right then. So I stared at the swirling, grey screen saver a little longer. Then I heard my Mom coming down the hall. She knocked on my door. "'Night, Will."

"'Night," I said. But I guess it came out quiet, because she put her head in my room, her face all pale and flat without her makeup on.

"Everything okay?" she asked.

I gave her a double thumbs-up and a stupid Disneyland grin. Mom rolled her eyes and shut the door. *Why*, I asked myself, *can't I have one moment where I do anything for real? Why's it all still a show?*

I listened a long time to Mom and Dad brushing their teeth in the bathroom. I wondered whether they think their life together is real or whether they, too, want a deeper connection. I heard them go into their bedroom, and then I didn't hear anything at all. There was just the sound of the neighbour's dumb dog — a slobber-mouthed Rottweiler. He kept barking and barking like it was the end of the world and wouldn't somebody come and save him? The Andersons kept that thing tied up to a tree in their backyard. And I guess they all wore earplugs to bed because the barking never seemed to bother them at all.

Chapter 4

Every queer person has a coming-out story, the moment where life forces a reckoning. If you ask my parents to tell you the story, they'll talk about finding gay porn on my computer. That horrible hour we sat at the kitchen table. My mother smiling, smiling her frozen smile. My father in his realtor suit, gripping the side of the table and saying, "Hold on. Just — just — just, hold *on*," as if the forward march of time was the problem. If they told you the story, they'd make themselves look more coherent, more loving. More prepared. But that's not the point. The point is that's not my coming-out story at all.

I don't think my coming-out story is even that time I told Julie when we got drunk on screwdrivers up at Cultus Lake. My real coming out was a week into the school year, when I borrowed my Mom's old Volvo station wagon and did the hour-long drive into Vancouver. I remembered the kids would make fun of the West End, "where all the faggots live." And when I Googled "Gay + Vancouver," stuff did seem to be ghettoized along a couple streets: Davie and Denman. You can only stare at other people's lives on a computer screen for so long before you get depressed. I wanted to see for myself.

I don't know what I was expecting. Unicorns shooting rainbows out their asses. Or just sun-dappled streets where happy gay couples roamed free. In fact, the West End was a mix of all kinds. Every block had a Starbucks where senior citizens were chatting up gay guys. And the locals were so packed in high-rises that the streets hummed with foot traffic. There were rainbow flags on some of the shop windows and Davie Street had rainbow banners hanging from the lampposts. But, as I trudged around, it dawned on me that nobody was about to step up and say, "Hi, you must be Will! We were waiting for you! This way to orientation."

I found this café called Delaney's. I camped out there — reading a science magazine, getting jacked up on coffee, hoping someone would talk to me.

Nothing. All these guys with their perfect hair and model bodies came in for lattes, laughing and patting each other on the butt. It made me want to press fast-forward and just *skip* the next few years, go straight to the part where I'm going to dinner parties with my doctor-husband.

And then, out of the blue, one guy *did* come up. He had this open grin and said, "Excuse me, can I give you my number? You're adorable." And he left a piece of folded paper on my table. *Adorable.* That's the exact word he used.

I mumbled, "Okay, thanks," like I was too interested in *Discover* magazine to notice him. I didn't even have the guts to take the number home. I knew I'd never call it, so I threw out the paper as I left the café. I tossed the first chance I ever had to connect with a guy.

Outside it was getting dark already. People were shouldering past me, annoyed because I was just standing there like a punching bag waiting for the next hit. I thought to myself, "At least that's a human contact . . . There's another . . ." while men in tight, clever T-shirts went hurrying home to slick condos in the sky. I was tired. I sat down on the curb. I don't know why, but I started to breathe really hard. And then, like a wuss, I was crying. Not just a couple tears, either. A big, shoulder-shaking, snot-running, oh-my-god-what's-wrong-with-me kind of crying.

And even as I was crying, I kept thinking, "Do I look adorable right now? Will somebody see me here and want to rescue me?" But the night just got darker, and I just became a patch of shadow on that hard curb.

Sometimes that happens. I think I'm doing fine and then a rope snaps inside my head and I fall apart.

Anyway, there was nothing I could do about anything then. I swiped at my eyes and walked back to Mom's beat-up station wagon.

That's my coming-out story, if you really want to know. It's me driving fast as I can away from friends and family toward a pack of strangers. And then it's me driving as fast as I can back.

Chapter 5

Julie was in a blow-up-the-world mood. She'd been thumbing through *Pride and Prejudice* one lunch down at the teacher's parking lot and reading parts out loud to me. Men with poncey names like Fitzwilliam and Bingley. Ladies drinking endless cups of sugary tea. She couldn't get enough of it. She read a paragraph out loud and threw the book down. "Why can't *we* live like that?"

"Like what? Like a bunch of repressed people?"

"*Elegant* people."

"Die of syphilis before you hit thirty . . ."

Julie stared. "In *Pride and Prejudice*, Will, if a man says, 'She's not handsome enough to tempt me,' he pays for it for 200 pages. In Chilliwack, guys can call a girl a dirty skank and then feel her up in the breezeway at lunch."

"Sounds like progress."

"Nice. Classy."

"Well, one of the few perks of being gay is you get to be a misogynist like crazy and nobody says anything."

Julie's a pretty girl. Even I could see that as she lay there on the little lawn beside the parking lot. She could have been with the cool kids if she wanted. But she found them boring, the way they encouraged dullness in each other, the way they talked about TV all day. Instead, she'd chosen to lie there with me, tapping at a page of *Pride and Prejudice* and willing the world to be made of better stuff.

"You know," she said at last, dog-earing her page, "everyone thinks I'm a lesbian now." She rubbed her shaved head and wriggled her eyebrows at me.

"It's a good-shaped skull," I said. "You've got small hands, too. So it's definitely an option if you're interested."

"Hmm." She was collecting mini daisies and had started to string them into a chain. "That might be just the thing to push my dad over the edge, actually."

She was always finding ways to bring him up. I gathered a few daisies for her and asked, "How many is he up to now?"

"Six beers on a good night. Twelve on a bad one."

"I guess that counts as official alcoholic territory, then."

"He doesn't get falling-down drunk, you

know? He just sort of fades into nothing every night around nine." She smiled faintly at the daisy chain in her hands and placed it in my hair like a crown. I loved her then. I loved her suddenly and accidentally and without any wish for it to be more than a sweet moment.

The moment got cracked, though, when Daniel Federline's penny loafers suddenly appeared beside our heads. I rolled up to a cross-legged position and said, "Oh, hello." He was looking down at us both like he couldn't possibly tell us the joke going on in his head.

"Don't you look something," said Daniel. He reached out to touch my daisy crown but I flinched away.

Then, in a move that changed everything, that invaded my little Julie world, he *sat down*. Of course he couldn't just sit. He had to brush the ground first, so no dirt would get on these red jeans he always wore.

He started unwrapping his lunch, which was all done up in different plastic compartments. Really anal. "So." He inspected a baby carrot. "How's everything been? I mean, with the great transition?"

"What are you talking about?" I was annoyed already. But I was pretty sure I knew what he meant.

"The change, darling! I mean coming out. Need any advice from an old queen?"

"Jesus."

"And I *am* an old queen, you know. I don't go in for this post-gay nonsense that the kids prattle about these days. I want drag queens and Judy Garland and *The Boys in the Band.*"

"The boys in what?"

"Oh, *Mary*," Daniel put his hand over his mouth and I could see he had white nail polish on. White nail polish with little stars bejewelled on the middle of each nail. Real fancy. "Do I need to write out a curriculum for you?" Daniel was getting going now, like he was on the makeover show Dad watches. "There's so much you need to digest! You should start by reading all six *Tales of the City* books. They're very retro, very 1970s, but that's where it all began, really. Then I've got a list of a dozen old movies you need to watch. They're all depressing as hell, and everybody dies of AIDS in the end. But, like I said, it's part of your *heritage.*"

Julie was no help. She was staring off, probably still thinking about her dad's beers chilling in the fridge. I told Daniel not to bother with his list.

"Oh, *I* see," he said. "*I* see. You're one of the post-gay kids, right? *Homo nouveau*?"

I started concentrating on throwing pebbles at the wheels of the principal's Buick. "I don't see why I have to become this new person just because I like guys," I said. "Most of who I am has nothing to do with who I hump."

"First of all, you're not humping *anybody*. I can *smell* the virgin on you. And secondly, I think you'll be surprised how much of your life is actually tied to your crotch."

"Maybe that's the way it is for you."

"Maybe that's the way it is for everyone. When you really dig down? When you get under why we have certain jobs, or wear certain clothes or talk to whom we talk to? It's all about sex."

"Don't say 'whom,'" I sighed. I was throwing full handfuls of pebbles now. Maybe I was scratching the car's paint a bit because Daniel grabbed my wrist to stop me. I shook him off.

He got the message and lay back — but not without whispering, "*Issues*."

Julie tried to swing things back to her dad, but Daniel angled in. He started rattling off all these websites with names like "Manhunt" and "Dudes-Nude." He was being nonchalant about it, too, like the names weren't pervy or anything.

I stopped him by throwing one of my pebbles at his face. "Are those porn sites?"

"You should have *said,* darling," he replied. "If you want porn sites I can give you a list of all the best ones. Although these days what you really want is a good aggregate site, something that collects the best videos from all the other sites."

"*These days*?" I gave him a sneer. "*These days*? Dude, you're seventeen."

"*Dude*?"

"You haven't exactly seen society *shift*."

Daniel batted his eyelashes and left it at that. And what can you say when a guy bats his eyelashes at you? There really isn't a comeback.

35

"Manhunt . . ." I sounded the word out real long, like it was Latin. "And you just upload your pictures and write about yourself?"

"And then, if you are me," said Daniel, "you log in every morning and sigh at an empty inbox."

"No bites, huh?"

"Well, when I first went on, when I was fresh meat, there were a few bites, yes. But nothing that was . . . up to my exacting standards. So I blocked anyone that looked like a waste of time. And now I don't get any messages at all. I've pretty much consigned myself to a life of spinsterhood."

"At seventeen."

"Well, if one is going to be a spinster, one might as well get on with it."

"Jesus, don't say 'one,' okay?"

"Why ever not?"

"Because it's faggy." Even as I said it, I knew I sounded like a jerk. But I'd been telling myself these things for so long. It was only when I said it to someone else that I realized how harsh it was.

If Daniel minded, he wasn't going to show it. He just gave me a whole lot of eyelash fluttering. "One *is* faggy," he said.

Then Julie decided to pipe up. She waved *Pride and Prejudice* in the air. "It's a truth universally acknowledged!"

Daniel and I both froze and looked over at her. "What's she about?" said Daniel.

"She wishes the world were written by Jane Austen."

"Ah, yes," said Daniel. "Then people like you and me could go to prison. Wouldn't that be fun. Oh, for simpler times."

Julie narrowed her eyes at Daniel. "Why don't you ask *Will* out, Daniel? Aren't you ignoring the simplest dating option for both of you?"

It's pretty much impossible to make Daniel Federline blush. But he did purse his lips even harder than usual, like he was spitting out lemon seeds. His Adam's apple was rubbing against the collar of his button-up shirt. I felt pretty bad for him. But I also didn't want to encourage him. So I just gave Julie this really ironic look. She got into that and gave me one back.

But I guess Daniel couldn't leave well enough alone. "Will is hardly my type, Julie-dear. I mean look at his *arms*. Noodles. Cooked noodles for arms. It wouldn't even *occur* to me to date such an ill-formed boy."

"Right." I half-rose and squatted in front of both of them. I flexed for Julie, and made sure Daniel could see plenty, too. Not like there were many muscles to flex. Daniel was right. But I knew it wasn't true about me not being his type. Any guy was Daniel's type because no guy would have him.

I said, "You're not exactly my type either, Miss Federline." That's what everyone used to call him back in junior high, when he first came to school wearing mascara. In grade nine, some kids pinned him down in the hall and wrote *Miss Federline* in black marker across his forehead. I remember running into him in the boy's bathroom after that. He was scrubbing soap into the words so hard he was panting. The rest of that day there was a black stain there.

"At least I've always known who I am," he blurted. "At least I'm self-*aware*." That really got me.

"Why are you even *here*, Daniel? Don't you have any friends?"

"I am here, Will, because, whether you know it yet or not, we queers have to stick together."

"Right." I'd had about enough of that. Besides, the bell was going to ring. I got up and held my hand out for Julie.

"And, no," said Daniel. "I don't have any friends." He fit all his lunch things back into a leather satchel, made a big show of getting up off the ground gracefully and walked away like a queen on a quest.

Chapter 6

Daniel might have been an ass, but he did have a way of getting a person thinking.

As the weeks went by and schoolwork dulled the spark of September, the idea of meeting someone online stayed with me. It was a teasing bright thing on the horizon. The rest of the world was making out in the sticky back row of the Cottonwood Cinema and I was sitting in my living room reading about Mars. I sure as hell wasn't meeting anyone on the streets of Chilliwack, where McDonald's hamburger wrappers blow down the sidewalks like tumbleweeds in a ghost town.

One weekend I took myself to the dehydrated park near my house and shivered on a bench, reading my magazine. One more story, I promised myself, and then you're going home to set up that profile. My mind kept drifting, though.

That morning I'd gone on YouTube and watched

the movie Daniel was going on about, *The Boys in the Band*. I just about decided to switch to girls then and there, if that's what being gay was going to look like. A bunch of catty queens ripping each other to shreds. These were the *friends* in the movie, these were the guys that *liked* each other. They were howling and abusing each other like it was a blood sport.

Truth is, I'd watched a couple of those movies Daniel was talking about. Up in my room, of course, with the headphones on. Really depressing stuff. And Daniel was right — everybody dies of AIDS in the end. But the part that really got me was that all these gay guys were middle-aged, or approaching it, and they didn't have any families. They all lived in tiny apartments in the middle of New York or San Francisco. They'd sleep around with men they scraped off the floor that night at the bar. They'd laugh and be real witty, but you could tell they were more weary than anything. It was like they'd made a mistake a long time ago and were going to pay for it by turning into lonely hunters.

But if I could find somebody now . . . If I could bypass that whole wrecked stretch of singleness . . . If I could find a way to be happier than all the sad men in the old movies. Daniel called me *Homo nouveau*, and maybe that's what I was. I wanted to find some new way of living that wasn't stained by the mess that came before — the AIDS, the oppression, the loneliness — all of it. Maybe

I'm a goddamn revolutionary.

While I sat there not reading a story about time travel, there came a too-loud voice behind me. "Well, if it isn't Will Johnson!" I turned around to see Adam Becker, arm around Laura as usual. You could tell he got a thrill out of saying it like that — "if it isn't Will Johnson!" — like he was in some old-time movie. Adam was the sort of guy that would be nice as hell if he ran into you away from school. Something about having a dad who was the top real-estate agent in town, I guess. Something about coming from a mega-religious family, too. Something about growing up in a place run by quiet, fierce faith.

"Hey, Adam. Hey, Laura." They were standing with the sun blazing behind them so I had to squint and shield my eyes.

"What're you reading?" Adam snatched at my magazine and flipped it around to see the cover, losing my place. "*Wonders of Science*! Sounds really fascinating, Will." He was getting sarcastic, smirking down at me. Laura sort of whispered in his ear and he let out a snort of laughter.

"It's been really charming to see you, Adam," I said. I wanted them to move along. I figured if I matched his fake tone, he'd get the hint.

But he gave me a face like I was being faggy instead of clever. "*Charming*? Yeah, Will, charming to see you, too." Then he looked down at Laura and sort of squeezed her shoulders even tighter. "You want to get going? Should we get you some hot chocolate?" He was baby-talking and she was lapping it up, cooing at him and leaning in. She should have had a soother in her mouth.

"See ya, Will." A switch had been flipped and he was friendly again, tossing the magazine in my lap and smiling his toothpaste-ad smile. I watched their backs as they crossed the park. I watched the way his shoulders stretched his denim jacket so you could see the muscles working. It was deep enough into the season that the leaves had started to fall, and Laura was kicking at them. Like a stupid kid.

I watched Adam's butt and thought about what he must look like in the shower after hockey games. Did he look like the guys in shampoo commercials? Did he give that big, close-eyed smile when he lathered up his hair? Did he — maybe — sneak a peek at the crotches of the other guys? And that made me crazy depressed, so I couldn't read at all. All I could do was watch the two of them get smaller and smaller as they walked toward the mall for Laura's hot chocolate. I guess I thought she was pretty lucky, to be able to act like some helpless child and just get taken care of, just get crushed under Adam's bulky arm.

I didn't feel like sticking around the park after that. So I rolled up my magazine and stuffed it in my back pocket. I headed home.

***

Mom and Dad were at a friend's place for dinner, which suited me fine. When they were gone I got to play house. I got a thrill out of walking through rooms in my underwear like a deadbeat dad on TV. I sat on the couch, felt the fabric on my thighs, and tried to imagine my dad sitting there in his underwear, too. He was always in that floppy grey suit, though. I tried to imagine him in an old gay movie instead — but his face wasn't as scrubbed as a gay guy's face. And his eyes weren't as anxious. His legs weren't as closed. Dad just wouldn't be a character.

"Brady Johnson gets to be just Brady Johnson," I said out loud. And once I'd said it, I realized I sort of hated him for it.

I ate my Kraft Dinner at the kitchen table while finishing up the time-travel story. Then I headed upstairs to stare down the Internet.

If you've ever Googled the words "gay dating," then you know most of the websites that come up are pretty raunchy. On a couple of them, the guys aren't even showing their faces, just their pecs and dicks. Which is pretty interesting to look at, I guess, but it seems like a terrible way to, say, find out what they think of *Battlestar Galactica*. I looked at those sites for a while and wondered why nobody had chest hair.

Eventually I found a site that was more my style. *ManTracker*. Sounds like a census or something. But it was all right. They had a no-naked-pictures rule that helped. I posted a few pictures that Julie had taken over the summer, shots of me floating in an inner tube, me climbing Grouse Mountain. Pictures of who I wanted someone to want me to be.

I had to write an About Me paragraph, too, and that was the worst. Then I had to fill out a bunch of stats, including my height, my weight, my hair colour and just about everything. One of the fields asked for "sexual position" and I put "versatile," which seemed the safest thing for someone who's never had sex at all.

One of the fields wanted "Your ideal first date." I thought about it a little and then pasted a link to a YouTube video: my favourite scene from the movie *Before Sunrise*. Way better than *The Boys in the Band*. It's just two strangers that meet on a train rolling through Europe. Two strangers — unfairly beautiful and bohemian — who can't stop talking to each other.

When I was done filling out the millions of intimate questions, I hit the Finish button. My profile went whizzing up to a satellite and bounced back to a server somewhere in the United States and, from there, it shuttled to thousands of computer screens belonging to thousands of men all around the world. *Click*. Sort of crazy.

"Now we play the waiting game," I said to nobody. Part of me expected something to happen right away. I guess I thought someone, somewhere would send me a message seconds later saying, "Finally, there you are! I've been *waiting* for you!" But that didn't happen. My profile just sat there among loads of other profiles. I saw myself become a tiny thumbnail photo, a headshot in a row. And there were rows and rows below my row. Up at the top of the window there was a bulletin that read, "688,256 guys are on ManTracker *RIGHT NOW*." I couldn't tell if that was supposed to be inspiring or what.

I looked at my profile for a little while. I tried hard to imagine what I would look like to a stranger. My profile was a little funny, but not in the way people are funny in those gay movies. Not witty. That made me pretty happy. If there was one thing I didn't want to be, it was *witty*.

All in all, the profile looked good. I would click it if I saw it there. All the boxes were filled in. None of the photos showed me behaving like a moron — a small triumph in itself.

Then, I don't know why, I started thinking about Adam and Laura. About the way they looked walking across the park. I thought about them with their arms around each other in the big, green world. I looked at my stupid laptop in my stupid room and it all looked as tiny and useless as a scene from a dollhouse. Adam would never post a profile of himself on some scuzzy dating site. He'd never sit alone in his room at his granddad's old wooden desk and spend a half-hour composing an About Me paragraph. He didn't go looking for love at all. It was somehow already part of his life.

Maybe, I thought, *maybe I'm already making that mistake, that mistake that all those middle-aged fags have made.* The mistake they didn't know they were making at the time, the one that made them all miserable and alone. Was I doomed already?

But what was the other option? There wasn't one. So I shut my laptop and went to bed. I lay there in my underwear, staring at the ceiling and thinking about the impossibility of time travel and Adam Becker's ass.

Chapter 7

Sometimes I wake up paralyzed. That's not a metaphor, either. I mean that I actually can't move at all for a minute. My mind will wake, but my body remains asleep. It's a condition called sleep paralysis. And I get it really bad.

Maybe once a month it comes. It's terrifying every time. But the embarrassing thing is the way I get out of it — I scream. I have to thrash my way to the surface, blast my body awake. So I try to scream, over and over. It takes a few tries. And then I'll get through and make this horrible strangled noise. My arms will sort of flail to life. I scramble up and out of bed then, because by that point I'm scared of lying down.

Because of the sleep paralysis, I understand why babies cry when you put them in their cribs. It's not the dark they're afraid of. It's the idea of sleep. They don't have any proof they're going to wake up again. They think they're going to die.

I had one of the attacks the morning after I set up my profile on ManTracker. I hollered out like an animal and collapsed off the side of my bed. That brought Mom pretty fast. She was at the door, poking her head in and chewing her lip. "Another one, eh?"

"I'm fine. I'm fine." She thinks of them as nightmares, which makes her babying me so much worse. I tried to explain once what it felt like, how it feels to be locked in your own body. She just said "Spooky," like I was describing a haunted house.

She came in and started pulling the sheets back on the bed. "You know," she said, "Doctor Wasserfall told me you don't have to scream when you come out of them. He said if you just wait it out, your body will wake up on its own."

Only someone with no idea what it's like would suggest you wait out a bout of sleep paralysis. It's like telling someone to stick their head underwater and breath normally. If I ever get married, the guy will just have to deal with the occasional blood-curdling scream. It wouldn't be the worst thing about me.

I told Mom I'd try to keep quiet next time and that made her happy enough. I'd already figured out that she just wants to feel like she's doing a good job as a parent. I'm not sure she cares how I turn out, as long as it isn't her fault.

Once the bed was made, she left me in peace and I remembered my ManTracker profile. Eight hours ought to be enough to hook a couple fish, I figured.

And I was right. There were six messages waiting for me. Here they are:

Sup.
Hey dude, I like your About Me.
Cute pics.
Sup.
Hey, how's your weekend?
Hey.

Maybe my expectations were too high. But I was pretty sure that if this were a romantic comedy starring Audrey Hepburn, she wouldn't respond to one-word ManTracker messages. If this were a romantic comedy, there'd be at least a paragraph. Or at least a good-looking guy behind the one-word message. But no. I clicked to their profiles and scrolled through photos of guys in their forties, baseball caps covering their bald heads. One of them I recognized as the guy who works at the Chevron station in town. A really gruff guy with sour breath who always sighs when you're just trying to buy a thing of Tic Tacs.

I decided to give it another day. Meanwhile, I had to finish *Pride and Prejudice* for English lit.

Top hats and tea parties filled half my Sunday. Every once in a while I'd raid the kitchen for some tea of my own and handfuls of biscuits my Mom buys because she thinks they look English.

After lunch, Julie called and said, "Just get

me out of this house." That meant her dad was having a really good time and was drinking more than usual. There was a hockey game on, so that figured. Julie and I decided to meet down at the Cottonwood Mall. It's in the ugliest part of town, but it's also where the Tim Hortons is. When Julie and I get together, it's important there is lots of coffee on hand. We both drink double-doubles and the conversation really flies.

We ended up sitting in our usual spot, in the alley behind the Safeway. I was doing my usual thing, flicking pebbles at the hood of the manager's pickup.

Julie sort of leaned back against this stone wall they've got there. She said, "I'm a stranger in a strange land."

"Hm?"

"Bob Dylan was singing that on the radio in Timmy's," she said.

Ever since she'd shaved her head, Julie was getting to be a real poet. I looked around the damp, broken-down alley, with its sewer grate clogged with decomposing maple leaves. Somewhere a mom was yelling at her kid to shut up about a birthday cake. I bit my lip. "Bob Dylan would be horrified," I decided, "if he knew his music was part of the Tim Hortons soundtrack."

"I think he'd love it," she said into her cup.

I shrugged. "You think Dylan was singing about Chilliwack?"

Julie ignored that one. She had a habit of

picking and choosing what she responded to. She put her drink up to her cheek to warm herself and looked as if she was waiting for me to ask about her dad. But I didn't feel like it. I was thinking about the inbox on my computer back home and wondering if my future husband was getting anxious.

"Thanks for getting me out of there," she said at last.

I gave in. "What's he like today?"

"Sort of slow and angry, like he's walking through melted wax. He moves around the house in his pajama bottoms like he's looking for something. But he ends up back on the couch watching the TV and shouting if anybody else makes a noise. He yelled at me for putting the groceries away too loudly. And meanwhile my Lola is howling at me from her bedroom 'cause somebody has to make her lunch."

"Hm."

"So that's when I called you."

"Your grandma's starving, then?"

"I made her some noodles."

"Did you think the guy in Timmy's was hot?"

"Are you even listening?" Julie threw me a look. I *was* listening. I always listen, sort of. But there's only so many times you can hear the same story. I was bored with her dad and his stupid, sweaty afternoons on the couch. It was all so predictable. Alcoholics are the most boring people in the world.

But she needed me to say something. So here's

what I said: "It's really not your problem, you know. A year from now you can be away at university, and then you'll only have to deal with them on holidays."

"They're my family, Will."

"So? Why should you condemn yourself to a lifetime of misery because of some accident of genetics?"

"So that's your advice? Run away and join the circus?"

"It's not running away. It's just growing up. Besides, I bet your dad would start taking care of your Lola if you up and left. You think you're chained to your family, but you're not. You think this is your life, but it isn't. I mean it. This . . ." I waved at the alley. "This is just the launch pad."

"For you, maybe." She made a face like she was deleting the rest of her thoughts.

"What's that supposed to mean?"

Julie stared at the back of the Safeway. "It means you've got a whole fabulous gay life waiting for you in the city. You're cute, you're smart." She turned toward me, took hold of my hand and started tracing the lines in my palm with her fingertip. "I'm going to read your future, Will, so listen. You're gonna end up living twenty stories in the sky with a view of the ocean. Because you're not *attached* — to this town or any place, or anyone. When you talk about your parents, if you *ever* talk about your parents, it will only be to bash them. And when you think of us, if you think of us, all this will look like a rehearsal for your real life. Your real life is going to start when you leave Chilliwack. But that's not the way it is for everybody." She dropped my hand. "This is where I'm going to be in ten years. My Lola's not going to stop needing me. My dad will never have the money to pay for university. This is my *life*. It's not a launch pad."

"So I'm destined to be an asshole." I wasn't too interested in her pity party.

"That's not what I said."

"It sure as hell sounded like that. It sounds like you think all gay guys grow up to be selfish pricks."

"Not *all* of them . . ." she mumbled.

I looked at my hand for a second, as though to check what she'd read there. I went back to tossing pebbles at the truck. "God," I said, "we should be smoking cigarettes if we're gonna talk like this."

"So my dad . . ."

I stopped her with a "Gah . . ."

"You know what, Will?" Julie stood up, suddenly red in the face. "You really don't get it. There's something *wrong* with you. There really is. Not everybody divorces their family. Can't you even look at me?" But I went on tossing pebbles. I don't know why people ever tell you to look at them. It's like ordering someone to kiss you.

I guess she stared at me for a little, waiting for I don't know what. But I just kept my eyes forward and waited for her to sit back down.

Julie wasn't calming down, though. She started shooting off about responsibility and Filipino
family life and sacrifice. And all I could do was
roll my eyes. She kicked a bunch of gravel at me
with her cheap rubber boots.

"Get over it, Julie!" I yelled. A piece of gravel
had lodged in my eye and hurt like hell. I stood up
and leaned over to try and dig the thing out.

"*You* get over it," she shot back. She chucked
her coffee cup against the back of Safeway before
disappearing down the alley.

***

Back at home my eye was still sore. On TV people
are always putting bags of frozen peas on black
eyes, so I decided I'd try that. But all we had was
half a bag of frozen fries. I could smell them when
I held it up to my face, sort of rank and pulpy. It
was gross. But I felt like feeling gross.

When my Mom saw me she switched on her
caretaker program. "Oh, honey! What *happened?*"

"Nothing." I really couldn't stand when she
was like that. But that didn't matter. She was doing it to make herself feel better, not me. I told her
a bug had flown in my eye.

"Well a bag of frozen chips isn't going to help
that," she said. "You need to do an eye rinse."

"It's *fine,*" I said. I went up to my bedroom with
the chip bag. It was thawing in my grip, though,
and water was dripping down my arm onto the

carpet. In my room I threw the thing away and sat down at my computer. If I pressed my knuckles into my eye hard enough it didn't hurt so bad. And I could still look at ManTracker with my one good eye. There was a new message.

Hey handsome,
I like the way you write; sounds like you've got a good head on your shoulders. A cute one, too. Anyway, send me a note if you'd like to chat sometime.
—Riley

He used a semicolon! Besides that, it was (just barely) long enough to count as a real letter. I clicked to his profile page. Sexy guy biking in a triathlon. Sexy guy drinking beer with friends. Sexy guy hiking through a sunlit forest. *Sold*.

But what to write back? I thought about it a long time, tried different openers. I wanted to show him I was interested, but I didn't want to freak him out with *how* interested. Wanted to look smart but not geeky. Funny but not a spaz. My whole future was hanging on this one message. I wrote:

Hey,
How's it going?

Brilliant.

Chapter 8

Daniel was his usual painful self at school Monday morning. He ambushed Julie and me at lunch in the teacher's parking lot. Maybe it was for the best, since Julie wasn't talking to me much since her blitzkrieg attack behind the Safeway.

Daniel picked up on the silent vibe pretty fast. He took it as a chance to launch a story-hour. "Last night," he said, "I went for my usual solo Sunday dinner at the Spaghetti Factory. But they weren't able to provide me with my usual table. My usual table being in the darkest corner, no overhead lighting or anything. I like to sit there and eat the chorizo penne real slow while reading a nice Barbara Pym novel or something." Daniel thought chorizo penne was the height of sophistication. I sighed and lay back on a bed of damp grass.

"*Anyhow*," said Daniel, "last night my usual seat was taken. So they placed me *right* in the middle of the room. Can you *imagine*?"

"I couldn't possibly," said Julie.

"*Right* in the middle. I was mortified. Mortified! And this big family sat down nearby. There must have been eight of them, all large and loud. Elbows-on-the-table types, you know? Teenage girls in kitten sweaters and everything. Well, I guess I started to stare. Purely out of anthropological interest. This strange family was something I was never going to be part of. And in that moment it just occurred to me how odd, how very *odd*, these people were. All bored with each other and stuffing their faces with complimentary bread sopping with garlic butter. Happy, I guess, in their monkey-like way. But just *pathetic* and . . . unaware of their own misery, I guess you could say."

"Could we?" Julie rolled her eyes at me. "This is where you're getting it from."

"Getting what from?" I asked.

"Your superiority complex. Your urban gay God attitude."

Daniel butted in before I could say anything. "And why not? Why shouldn't we feel a sense of superiority? After decades of oppression, it's finally obvious to the elite — not here in Chilliwack, mind you, but out there, out there in the *city* — that gay men are superior in looks, intelligence, and charm."

"Real charming," said Julie. "And is it just the guys that have this bonus, do you figure? Or are lesbians superior, too?"

"Well," sniffed Daniel, "*lesbians*. Anyhow, back to the family of monkeys. I guess one of them, the father, saw me staring. And I guess I *happened* to be staring, in that moment, at their elder son."

I tossed Daniel a look. "You're *always* staring at guys."

"*Anyhow*. The father got this horrible, screwed-up look on his face, which was turning the colour of cranberries, I swear. He actually leaned over his chair and muttered at me, 'Eyes on your own table, princess.' I don't need to tell you how embarrassing *that* was. I couldn't even finish my spumoni. I fled. I just fled."

It was hard not to feel sorry for Daniel, even if he was an ass. I knew he didn't mean to be a creep or anything. He just sometimes wasn't aware of the impression he was making. He was pretty caught up in his own world. And I could appreciate that, because sometimes I feel like everybody else is just an extra, like their lives aren't as real as mine. Maybe everyone feels that way a little.

Daniel fussed with his collar and decided to change the topic. "Did you try any of those websites I told you about?"

"Oh, Will," Julie was tilting her head at me and giving a disapproving look. "You're not cruising online are you? That's so . . . *pedestrian*."

"What's the alternative, Julie? Sorry it's not how people meet in nineteeth-century novels." I was still pissed about the day before. And now she was starting up about something she knew nothing about. "It's not like I can just walk down the hall asking guys out, you know."

"Right," she mumbled, "because that's what I do."

I turned to Daniel, ignoring her. "Anyway, yeah, I did sign up for one. For ManTracker."

"Of *course* you'd pick ManTracker," said Daniel. "The safe one with no dick pics."

"Whatever. It worked. I got a message from a nice guy." I was saying it out loud because I wanted to hear myself say it. But of course, once I'd begun, Daniel was all over me with questions and critiques. "You've *got* to ask him out, Will. If he made the first move, it's only proper etiquette."

"He's older than I am," I said. "So I figure he's in charge of at least the first date." It felt sort of good to be strategizing. Julie and I had strategized about her dates a hundred times before.

"No dice," said Daniel. He started packing up his plastic lunch containers with the deliberate, fine-china way he had. "You being younger probably intimidates him. If you don't ask him out, he's not gonna have the balls to do it himself."

"Wait, wait, wait," said Julie. "How much older is this guy?"

"He's twenty-three."

"Twenty-three! Is that even, like, *legal*?"

"I'm pretty sure it's legal, yeah."

"Twenty-three's the perfect age for you," said Daniel, giving me a grandma hand-pat. "He'll be

59

able to teach you things. He'll be able to teach you . . . techniques."

"Oh, gross." With that, Julie went off to social studies. Daniel and I stood up and watched her go.

"She's doing that a lot lately," I said. "Storming off."

"Just wait till you get a boyfriend," said Daniel. "Then she's going to have to deal with not being the centre of your world."

"Hm." We started walking after her, toward the rear of Spencer High.

"But do ask this man out," said Daniel. He linked his arm through mine for a few steps, like we were characters in *Pride and Prejudice*. I surprised myself by not pulling away. But as we got close to the school, Daniel's self-preservation kicked in and he let go on his own. He was quiet for just a few steps, a century in his world. "That dad at the Spaghetti Factory called me a fag, by the way. Not princess."

"Hey?"

"When I was staring at his son and he caught me. He turned around and said 'Eyes on your own table, you little faggot.' If he'd just called me a princess, I would've given him a curtsy and forgotten all about it."

"That sucks."

"Yes, Will, it does." Daniel stopped walking and fixed his scarf, which he had tied in some elaborate knot under his jacket. "So when I tell you to go on a date with a nice guy from ManTracker, it's not just because I think you need to get some action — although I do think that. It's because the world is still full of hateful, ignorant people. And if you don't grab at the occasional nice guy, you're going to miss out."

"Good advice," I said.

"I know." He looked up at the cracked, grey walls of the school and got quiet again. Only for a second. Then it was kiss-kiss, fluttery eyes and, staring me down, he said just one word (with a French accent) — "*Courage*." And off he flew.

It still sounded like good advice when I went up to my bedroom that night after dinner. I wrote Riley another note and asked him on a proper date. Nothing clever, nothing witty.

Then I went downstairs and sat between Mom and Dad on the couch to watch *Glee*. When I looked at either one of them, the blue light from the TV gave them blue alien skin. They were staring ahead as if they were asleep with their eyes wide open.

Chapter 9

Date night! After school on Friday, I told Julie I had to stay home with my parents for a family night. Then I told my parents I was catching a horror double-bill with Julie at the Cottonwood Cinema. Bases covered.

On the drive out to Vancouver, I worked my way through Mom's stash of *Hooked on Classics* tapes, which she kept crammed in the glove compartment. Ninety minutes and three tapes later, I was walking down a tree-lined street toward a café on the edge of Stanley Park. It took me forever to find parking, so I was rushing and feeling pretty frazzled. I had my phone out and was trying to look up a picture of Riley that I'd downloaded. Not that I was so sure it'd be any help. People lie.

But I knew him right away. Strange to walk up to a half-known stranger. He had on this beat-up hunting jacket with extra pockets down the front.

He was leaning back on the heels of his boots scanning the block down the other way. He had a scruffy bit of beard, too, which he didn't have in the photos. The first thing I thought was that this guy didn't look gay at all. I guess that's a terrible thing to say, but it's what I thought. Frankly, if he *had* looked like my idea of a gay guy, I might have walked away.

When he spotted me, he tossed me this lop-sided grin like we were both in on a secret, which I guess we were. He stuck out a hand to shake. "Will? Hey, I'm Riley." This guy was going to take the lead, and that suited me fine. As far as I was concerned, I was an observer, like those guys on nature documentaries who talk all quiet and hushed while animals start eating each other.

We grabbed a couple coffees and got to walking the seawall that circles the park. As the light failed, I could begin to see 10,000 smug, twinkling homes on the other side of the water in West Vancouver. I was hungry as hell and kept scrounging pieces of an old oat bar out of my pocket like an idiot.

Walking was a good idea because I could go along without saying anything, like I was taking in the sunset or something. Riley filled the silence, anyway, with talk about his work at a "real estate activation agency."

"You're a realtor?" I asked.

"I don't like that word," he said. "I help people find their homes."

"So, a realtor," I said.

He shrugged.

"My dad's a realtor." The moment I said it, I bit my lip and looked away.

"Oh yeah?" Riley didn't notice the creep factor. He started telling me a bunch of stories about the ad people in his office and how they all fuss about "banal details like they're saving the world . . . We had a two-hour meeting, I'm not kidding, about whether or not we should include dogs in the pictures showing the inside of a condo we're trying to sell."

I said it sounded pretty soul-crushing and asked what they decided in the end.

"They decided to *try* it. The senior director said we had to do the shoot with and without the dog so he could have both options. This is thousands of dollars, you know? Thousands of dollars that go into pictures of fancy condos when it could have been spent sending a bunch of African girls to college or something." He shook his head and did a "what're-you-gonna-do?" face.

I said I doubted the money would go to African girls if they didn't spend it on photo shoots. But Riley said that wasn't the point, that it was the principle of the thing.

"What principle?" I said.

"The principle of making things *count*," he said, waving an arm out at the ocean to our right. "The principle of thinking that what we do *matters*, that people should be working toward a better planet, not just making a buck. Or spending a buck." It's pretty sexy watching a guy get worked up about his beliefs, even if they're sort of lame.

"Is that what you're doing there?" I asked. "I mean, does that work count for you?"

He gave me that lopsided grin again and shoved his hands in his pockets. "It's what I'm *going* to do that matters. The agency is just a stepping stone. Eventually, I'm going to do more serious things."

"Like what?"

Riley told me that wasn't really the point, either. But he rattled off a few causes he had, and started talking about something called "urban planning" and how the design of a city could change the people living there.

I said I liked that idea. It was like the way a person's feelings weren't really his fault but just part of a big system. Like the city was an enormous breathing animal and we were just the bacteria living inside of it.

Riley said no, that wasn't it at all.

After a couple hours, it was getting dark enough to make me better looking. It was handsome dark. The seawall was almost abandoned. Riley was zigzag walking and bumped into me a couple times, which I didn't mind. He wasn't what I'd dreamed about, of course. He wasn't near enough my age and he talked in a breezy, sure way, like there was no difference between selling houses and nighttime seawall chatter. Under the sexy coat, his chest was straining against a fluorescent green Abercrombie & Fitch shirt that I silently disapproved of. Still, he wanted to touch me and that was a small miracle. He had a good six inches on me in height. It got my heart thumping to think a guy, older and bigger, was interested.

We decided to sit on the ledge of the seawall and watch a lit-up freighter cruise by. It was quiet, except for the tide working at the rocks beneath our feet. The water was ink black, as black as the night sky above. If it weren't for those twinkling houses on the other side of the harbour, there'd have been one spread of dark from the water up into space.

I wanted to get the conversation off my family, which Riley had been asking about. So I started telling him about how the light from stars takes millions of years to reach the Earth, how looking at those stars is like looking way back in time. I said the stars we see might not even exist anymore.

"I did actually know that already," said Riley. I guess I looked embarrassed, because he put his hand on my thigh and said, "It's cute, though, that you're into that stuff. I mean, I like that you're a bit of a geek. Most guys your age only talk about viral videos or how drunk they got last weekend."

"Thanks." I wasn't sure how to take that, but at least he was smiling. I rubbed the back of my neck — so corny, but it seemed like the thing to do. Really bashful, you know?

"Anyway," Riley stood up and looked toward

the city's lights. "You wanna head back?"

"I've got to make a couple phone calls," I lied. It seemed like a nice end for the evening, if he went off and I got to stare at the sky some more. Besides, I knew I'd just mess things up if I had to walk back into town with him.

"Okay," Riley said. "Give me a hug, then." I'd never been hugged like that by a guy before. It was none of this rough pat-pat, shoulder-slapping stuff people at school do. He sort of held me tight with one hand while the other moved up and down along the back of my jacket. I actually had to cut the thing short because I was getting hard and didn't want him to feel it through my jeans.

"G'night," I said, stepping back.

He gave me a wrinkly smile straight out of a movie and said we'd talk soon. Then he leaned in and brushed my cheek with his lips — so, so lightly I wasn't sure it had happened, or whether I could even call it my first kiss from a man. I watched him walk away for a bit before remembering to take out my phone and pretend to call someone.

Once he'd gone, I sat some more on the edge of the seawall. It was a good place for looking at the stars and thinking about aliens. You need a very quiet place to really think about outer space. You need to feel like you're almost floating in space yourself, like there's no way some idiot's gonna come and ask you for a cigarette.

I wanted to give myself a good long time to

think about communicating with aliens. I thought about what the conversation would be like. We'd blast a "Hey" from some laser canon. Then, 10,000 years from now, our ancestors would get a "Hey, what's up?" shooting back at the speed of light. Intergalactic text messages.

People talk about "direct communication" but, of course, that's impossible. Even when you read a great poem in English class, and you think *That's it, that's exactly how to describe that*, you realize a second later it's not *exactly* it, after all. It's never quite what a guy means.

I silently asked the ocean if Riley would be my boyfriend. I used telepathy to tell it that I had no clue, none, about what I was doing, that Riley might be a good one or an evil one. But that all I wanted for starters was *someone*. And shouldn't I have a go? The water didn't give me anything back. Eventually I started shivering, so I made my way back to my mom's car for the long drive home.

Chapter 10

About a week before Halloween, Julie and I decided to go on one last hike up in the woods around Cultus Lake. All summer, the campgrounds are filled with yahoos getting drunk on cheap beer. They really rip the place up, those boys. They jump through fires in their underwear and shout their heads off. Last summer, a kid got killed when someone came back to camp with extra beer and drove his car straight over an occupied tent. When you see how crazy those guys get, it makes you wonder whether it's their weekday lives that are the fake. Maybe they're just pretending to be civilized when you see them wearing ties and eating cheeseburgers in the window at Burger King. Maybe what they really want to do is rip off all their clothes and start throwing things around.

Anyway.

Those guys don't go up to the lake in October,

not when the nights get cooler. So Julie and I had the woods to ourselves that afternoon. It was pretty. The clouds were gone for once. The sun was slanting through the trees and lighting up the leaves like they were a 3D cartoon. I liked being up there. I told Julie it would be a good place to head if there were ever a zombie apocalypse.

Julie turned and said, "What do you mean *if*?" She started hiking up the trail again but kept on talking. "The zombie apocalypse happened a long time ago, buddy. Walk through the Cottonwood Mall and tell me it's not full of zombies. It's you and me against the walking dead."

We talked a while longer about zombie survival skills, and then Julie started talking about her dad again. He was drinking even more than usual, she said. Yadda yadda yadda. I tried to act sympathetic, but it's hard to care when someone keeps complaining about the same thing.

Finally Julie must have worn herself out because she went dead quiet.

"So I went on a date," I blurted. And then I snatched at some branches, which made a ton of dead leaves come down on our heads like it was snowing brown.

"Jesus, Will." Julie swatted at the bits that stuck like Velcro to her buzzed head. She didn't seem too interested in my date, but I guess she figured she had to ask. "Who with? With that old guy?"

"Not old. Riley's twenty-three. He lives in the city."

"*Riley?*"

"Yeah. He's a realtor."

"A *realtor?* Oh, Will . . ."

"You can be such a snob, you know that?"

"So what's he like, then?" She was breaking twigs into little bits as she walked.

"Sort of . . . blank, I guess. He doesn't read much. He's more about the now. He's a happy guy."

"And Riley's twenty-*three?*" I told her yes and Julie said, "Are you *fersure* sure that's legal?"

"God, Julie! Yes. Legal. Legal and nice."

"Well, even if it's legal, I don't think . . ."

"Maybe just don't think about it then, okay?" I pushed past her on the trail. I was sick of looking at the back of her head.

"I'm just looking out for you," she called. "I'm just saying you don't have to *settle* for—" Her voice sounded hurt but I stopped listening.

The air had shifted and now the woods didn't seem like such a great place after all. I looked around at dead leaves everywhere, at roots cracking out of the dirt path. You could see through the trees sometimes, and the valley below had a muddy smudge around it, thanks to the smog that blows in from the city and gets stuck there. Nature's really a mess if you're not in the mood for it. I told Julie I felt like heading back, and we walked to the car without talking about much at all.

I guess my mood was shot then. All night, I looked at my dad watching TV, or my mom

71

working on some stupid crafts at the kitchen table. All I could think was *Get me out of here*.

***

I should say I wasn't doing a great job of getting myself free from Chilliwack, though. I was called in to the school counsellor's office over my wobbly grades, in fact. There, I was subjected to twenty minutes of Mr. Bernstein's thick-tongued conversation. He was a large man, maybe 250 pounds, and smelled of cabbage and Irish Setter. He wore moth-eaten Bill Cosby sweaters with jagged geometrics all around them. You couldn't help but stare at his wool-wrapped belly when he talked at you. "These grades, Will . . . I don't know . . ." He was scrolling through my transcript on his laptop and taking big sticky breaths through his mouth. "They certainly . . . they aren't going to get you an early admission to UBC. And it looks like that's . . . Yes, that's the only school you applied to. Do you think that was wise? Putting all your eggs in one basket?"

"I guess not."

"Mmm."

We stared at each other for a minute while I thought about the afternoon I'd filled out my UBC application. It had felt like a massive effort to even get that done. It felt like my future couldn't possibly be determined by filling out forms, or doing well on tests, or anything I was doing now. Here was Mr. Bernstein peering at me in his cramped, fluorescent-lit office, with a poster behind his head that read, *"You Are Your Own Destiny."* I thought, *What the hell can that possibly mean?*

Chapter 11

When Riley found out I didn't know how to swim, he made it his mission to teach me. I said that sounded like a productive way to hang out and he laughed like I was being clever.

The YMCA in downtown Vancouver is pretty swank. Riley signed us up for something called the Men's Plus membership, which meant "free towels and no gross poor people." Ooh la la.

In the change room, I had a hell of a time finding a way to get into my swimsuit without exposing myself too much. Lots of guys were walking around naked. The image of their junk bounced around on all the mirrors so the same dick came at you multiple times. Riley filled his locker with clothes and sat naked, wide-legged on the bench. He took his time digging his swimsuit out of his backpack — a skimpy, cherry-red thing that snapped against his skin as he shoved himself into it.

Out in the pool, I was a disaster. Riley sat on the edge of the slow lane and dangled his feet in the water while I jumped in. He told me to do a practice lap so he could check my technique. I told him I didn't have any technique, I just flailed around. But he said not to worry. So I chugged down the lane and back, taking breaths whenever I felt like I was about to pass out.

When I was done, I pushed my hair back and looked up at Riley. He nudged my chest with his foot and said, "You really are pretty terrible at that." But he had a big grin on his face, so I assumed being terrible at something was cute.

Riley started giving me tips. I did another lap and then another. I could feel a tiny improvement right away. And I realized I sort of liked the idea of swimming. I liked that it was just me and the water. I liked the idea of a sport that didn't involve a team. I liked how exhausted it made me feel, how it cleared my head of all the buzzing and left me just counting: one, two, breathe . . . one, two, breathe . . .

After a half-hour I was gulping for air. Riley took me back to the Men's Plus locker room. Once the door locked behind us, he shucked off his swimsuit with a little sigh, the same sigh my mom uses when she steps out of her high heels. He slopped his suit onto his shoulder and looked back at me. "Wanna have a steam before we head out?" I followed him past a hot tub, which looked like a shrimp cocktail with all those floating pink faces peering up at us. I grabbed a towel and wrapped it around me, tight.

The steam room reminded me of the first two minutes of a porno. Through the sweaty air I could see a half-dozen guys, some buck naked, some with towels like me, sitting on a sort of raised bench. Their faces were hard to make out in the rising steam, but their crotches were — painfully — in view. We sat down and Riley started chatting up the guy beside him.

I stared forward. There was an old guy there, maybe seventy, with big drooping breasts and a tired little mushroom dick. He looked sad, with his face all red and blotchy from the heat. He was looking down at his feet, which were strapped into black plastic sandals. Once in a while he would sneak a look at one of the younger men up on the bench. Then he'd return his gaze to his hairy toes, his puckered fingers. I guess I felt sorry for him. But it got so hot in there you couldn't think about anything for long. I lay my head against the tiles on the wall and waited for boiling hot drops to fall from the ceiling and scour my chest.

Afterward, out on the sidewalk, I asked Riley about the old guy. "You mean the Creep?" he laughed. "Omigod, that guy spends hours in the steam room every day. I've seen straight guys yell at him for looking at their dicks. He doesn't even use the weights or the pool. He just hangs out in the steam room and peeks at men. But don't worry, he's harmless."

I thought about the old man some more while

we walked down to Riley's favourite noodle place. I thought about how the Creep spent all that extra money to get the Men's Plus membership, just to sit in a room with a few naked men. How he never touched any of them, but wanted to be there, just wanted to *see*. I thought it was just about the saddest thing I'd ever heard.

***

By the end of November, Chilliwack was looking even smaller than usual. You wouldn't understand if you grew up in a city. But if you're raised in the boonies, and then discover a new life in a city — a *real* city where they've got more than one sushi place and guys walk down the street holding hands — well, you just can't go back.

I told mom I'd discovered a "coming-out club" in Vancouver. In a way, it was true. It did the trick anyway. Mom and her clubs. "Good for you, Will! *Good* for you!" And she promised I could have the car every Friday to trek out there.

Julie and I were getting into pointless arguments every lunch hour, both of us convinced we'd somehow been betrayed. And Daniel Federline wasn't much better. Julie and Daniel would sit, munching on their sandwiches and acting like the biggest thing in the world was what somebody said in math. I just couldn't stand it. I'd try to talk about Vancouver, or Riley, or the future. But they'd just grow quiet, as though I'd put them down.

In the end, I guess Julie got sick of me rolling my eyes. One day she yanked her toque down tight over her head and said, *"God* you need to stop talking about Riley. Riley, Riley, Riley."

Daniel was fixing the fold on the cuffs of his jeans so they would look "more imperfect." He gave a little nod after Julie's announcement. "I'm afraid I agree, darling. You're obsessed. It's not becoming."

"Why do you guys want to take this away from me?" I could hear my voice going sour, but I couldn't help it. "When I'm finally connecting with somebody? When I've *finally* got a chance to try living?"

Julie curled her legs up against her chest. "What do you mean, finally connecting with somebody? Who am *I*, Will?"

I couldn't take it. "You're really going to pretend it's the same thing when you've got dozens of guys at this school you can date whenever you want? Listen, all I want is a taste of a real life, instead of this . . . limbo. This boring, shitty town." They weren't talking now, either of them. "It's only been a couple months, anyway."

"Exactly." Daniel leaned back into Julie's legs. They'd been getting closer in my absence. "You're smitten on nothing. Suddenly, you drive into the city all the time. And when you *are* in Chilliwack, you're at the rec centre. Doing what? Picking up more men?"

"I'm swimming," I said. "And before you ask, Julie, yes, swimming's legal."

She gave me a look. "The point, Will, is that you've obviously changed your priorities. And Daniel and I aren't on the new list."

"You know what, Julie? You don't get it. You can't possibly understand what being gay in a piss-ant town like this means. I can't *live* here, do you get that? I can't *live* here." I ripped out a bunch of dead grass and started tearing it into tiny pieces of green confetti.

"Like you have any idea what it's like to be Filipino in this Wonderbread factory? Besides," Julie said, "Daniel lives here and he's gay."

I sniffed. "Daniel's not living. You're basically not gay if you aren't doing something with another guy. And I'm out there, Julie. I'm actually *doing* it."

Daniel's smile was hard and tight and it made me feel suddenly sick. "It's true," he said, to the ground. "I'm like the crazy best friend in a movie. Everybody else is having a *thing* happen to them, a real *thing*, and I'm just there to fill out the crowd."

"As *if* you've blended into a single crowd in your life," said Julie.

We all pretty much stared at the ground after that. Finally, Daniel broke the silence by standing up, buttoning his yellow coat and saying, "It's getting too cold to eat lunch out here, kids. I'm going to start eating in the cafeteria. Julie?"

She got up and followed Daniel back to the school. I watched them go. They looked small and helpless in their too-big winter coats, like a couple of kids.

Chapter 12

The days, the weeks, slipped by. Riley and I settled into each other's lives, or I settled into his. I let myself forget about my grades and my desperate university application. When I took that long arrow of a highway into the city, it felt like I did have a future. And for a little shining time Riley's friends (loud, smart, and dressed in perfect pink polo shirts) became my friends. A pack of us would go to movies, to the new pizza place, or out for beers. And when I took the highway home again, my new life was put on pause. There was one world and then there was the other. And the only connector was me and the lies I told my mom in order to borrow her car — my rickety spaceship.

One day I was in town, waiting for Riley to get off work, so I went for a swim at the Y. I'd just finished a couple laps and was resting at the end of the lane when a pair of feet stopped in front of me. I looked up and saw one of Riley's friends, Matt, looking down at me with a funny expression on his face. I'd met Matt a couple times before. Mostly I'd be quiet at group things, but Matt had been pretty nice, finding ways to include me in the conversation.

He looked down at me from the pool deck and said, "You look like a David Hockney painting in those white trunks."

"A what?"

"David Hockney. Famous gay painter? Liked to paint gorgeous young men dashing around underwater? Hockney! No?"

I shook my head. "Must be before my time."

"Oh, puh-lease — no excuse. Hockney is before my time, too. Actually, he might not be dead yet . . . Either way, a little bit of queer history would be an idea."

"You sound like Daniel Federline from my school."

"Daniel Federline sounds like a smart child."

I didn't have much to say then, so I just smiled up at him. He was wearing a black Speedo and had these bright blue goggles strapped around his neck. "Listen," he said, "some of us are going for a drink in an hour. Why don't you join? I'll text Riley and get him to come meet us."

"Dee-lightful," I said. It was a strange thing for me to say, and it sort of freaked me out when I heard it come out of my mouth.

Matt just nodded down at me and pulled his goggles up over his eyes so he turned into a kind of alien. I kicked away into the water.

***

At the pub, I sat down with Matt and a couple other guys I hadn't met before. They didn't bother to introduce themselves, figuring they'd never meet me again. There was a tall one and a bald one. They both spent most of the evening sucking on bottles of beer and looking around like they thought a movie star was about to walk into the place.

"Will's been dating Riley," offered Matt.

"Oh yeah?" said the bald one. He looked at me sidelong and raised his bushy eyebrows.

"Yup," I said.

"You do know that he's . . . Well, I mean, you *are* being safe, right?"

I guess my ears turned red or something. Matt leaned forward and tried to derail the conversation. "Of course they're safe. You kids these days, you know all about your condoms, don't you?"

I rolled my eyes. But I didn't want to admit to some asshole that Riley and I hadn't had sex yet. So I told the bald guy, "Things are under control." Matt laughed at that. The bald guy raised his eyebrows again, but was looking over my head at a big man in a hoodie who had just walked in. "There's a man I'd like to have under my control . . ."

The campy thing he was doing reminded me of Daniel Federline. It reminded me of all those old gay movies too. *Such a faggy way of acting*, I thought. And then my mind twisted around on itself in reproach. I couldn't tell whether I was upset with my own thoughts or with the things that had inspired them. Either way, I really couldn't stand it.

The tall one leaned in and started picking through a bowl of peanuts on the table. "And how long has this been going on?"

"Couple months," I said. It felt good to take a gulp of beer whenever I said anything — like drinking was the period at the end of sentences. So I took a big swig and looked around myself.

"Well then," said the tall one. "This *is* serious."

I wasn't interested in going into things with them, so I started asking about movies. I don't really like talking about movies. But when I'm stuck talking to a table full of guys like that . . . We went on talking about Ryan Gosling ("So divine," said the bald one) and James Franco ("He can do anything," said the tall one) for maybe twenty minutes. But then our beers were done and the conversation seemed to be drained, too.

I looked at the pub's front door just as Riley finally arrived, bundled up in his old hunting coat. There was snow melting in his crazy hair and the cold had made the tips of his ears turn red. I thought he was better looking than any other guy on the block. He came stomping over to our table and planted a kiss on me like we'd been boyfriends forever. Those warm, chapped lips. I could feel his smile broaden as his mouth worked on mine, as though kissing were a joke. My hand went up, in a reflex, to feel his chest through his snow-dampened shirt. I realized as it was happening, in that very moment, that it was the first time I'd ever kissed a guy in front of other people. It felt like a billboard had suddenly appeared above us, reading *Will Johnson is Kissing a Man! On the Mouth!* But nobody broke out into applause. They just started talking about James Franco again as if the world hadn't changed at all.

As he sat down, Riley patted his breast pocket and said, "You guys ready to have some fun tonight?"

"Actually, I'm out," said Matt. As he walked around the table, he leaned toward me and gave me a friendly peck on the cheek. "You be careful, now."

Chapter 13

"Fun" is a funny word. I'm used to getting drunk on cheap beer, and I'm used to sharing a joint now and then. But these guys were in another league. Their idea of fun included cocaine, a fact that surprised me less than the fact that Riley was the guy providing the stuff. He tugged not one, but two baggies out of his pocket a few minutes after we arrived at the bald one's penthouse.

"I'm house-sitting for Gore Vidal's house-sitter," declared the bald one. He collapsed into a crowd of purple pillows that had been left like a nest on the couch.

Riley smirked and said, "It's true, you know, it's true," as we sat ourselves on the rug opposite the bald one. The tall one was already in the kitchen mixing cocktails. "Something lemon . . . something sweet . . ." He was fiddling with bottles and dashing things into a martini shaker.

I leaned back on my hands and watched as Riley took out a credit card and a business card and started working the drug into tiny lines on the glass coffee table. They made *chip-chip-chip* sounds as he tidied his work. I'd never taken anything up my nose before and wasn't especially looking forward to it. *Virgin nose*, I thought to myself. I saw Riley smirk at me with a look he'd never used before, a cross between fatherly interest and brotherly exasperation. "You don't have to, you know," he said.

"I didn't say I didn't want to. I've never done it before, that's all."

He shook my knee lightly with one hand and said in a singsong voice, "Well, don't go corrupting yourself on *my* account."

But I told him I wanted to try. More to the point: I wanted to try being part of what was going on here. An adult, almost glamorous evening, far from the lame smuggled beers that made up a night in the abandoned playgrounds of Chilliwack. Which is not to say there wasn't plenty of blow in the Wack. Drug dealers love bored suburbanites. But the tiny unit of Julie and me was never enough to attract the sort who would offer.

Riley gave me another smirk and said, "Well, I think you ought to go first, you know. A place of honour."

I craned around to watch the tall guy re-emerge from the kitchen, carrying a tray of muddy looking cocktails.

"This is good stuff," Riley cooed, to reassure me. "Nothing nasty cut into it, I mean. It's exactly what you'd want as a first-timer." Riley rolled up the business card he'd been using and handed it over.

"Don't you use rolled up money or something?"

A chorus of pshaws. "Disgusting," said the bald one. "So dirty."

I saw myself for a moment, superimposed on a scene from one of those sitcoms where the teenage girl has to stand up to her drug-crazed friends. But when it came to it, I couldn't find the energy to care about anything so clichéd as peer pressure. Almost on autopilot, I leaned forward with the rolled-up card, shut one nostril with my index finger and snorted a line with gusto.

"Atta boy!" Riley rubbed my back.

I smiled up at him, rubbing my nose. "How long does it take?"

"Not long." Riley was worrying over the lines some more, like a mother making sure everyone gets a fair slice of birthday cake. The others did their lines with businessman faces. I was glad to see they were doing it the way I had; the movies I was copying hadn't failed me. Leaning back on my hands again, I watched the bald one pick up some white remains with his finger and rub the drug onto his gums. I looked around at us, at the slick glass apartment. *This is cool*, I thought. *We're pretty damn cool. Other people? Idiots, mostly. But us, this — this is pretty cool.*

As the others started talking about people I didn't know, I noticed the upright piano in the corner. I'd had taken lessons when I was a kid, and I was pretty sure I could still play. In fact, I was pretty sure I might be a bit of a genius at the piano. I walked over to it. The guys watched me plunk myself down and start fiddling with the keys. I was pretty impressed with the sound I was making. So I was all the more pissed off when the tall guy drowned me out by putting on some numbing house music.

We all did another line, maybe twenty minutes after the first. I started nodding at Riley, saying, "Yeah, yeah, I think I can feel it."

"You *think*?" he said. He was rubbing his stomach and his pecs in a strange figure-eight, like he was petting himself or feeling himself up.

I wanted to tell them about space then, about time travel and black holes and dark matter. Everything I'd ever read in a science magazine was coming back to me at once and I couldn't quite *tell* them how things worked, because I just knew too much. There was so much to explain. One truth was overlapping with other truths and stamping up my throat and out my mouth at once, until they were laughing and laughing and I was left saying, "No, you *guys*! You *guys*!" Which only made them laugh more.

I asked to do a third line. And then a fourth. After my fifth, Riley had me seated between his legs on the floor, with his hands up my shirt, and he was mumbling dirty things in my ear. The hornier he got, though, the more I started to feel gross. I drank some water to calm myself down. Riley said, "Let's share a Viagra." At that point, I would have swallowed anthrax if he'd suggested it. I popped half the little blue pill and, while I was still gagging on its edges, Riley announced that we were leaving.

The bald one looked over from a deep conversation he was having with the tall one on the couch. He said, "Understood," before turning back to the tall one and saying, "But if Chris had only read *The Secret* like I *told* him to, this sort of thing wouldn't happen to him . . ."

Riley and I slipped out the front door of Gore Vidal's house-sitter's penthouse. We took the elevator twenty stories down to the blacked-out street. I started panicking about getting the car home, so Riley took my phone and texted my mom that I was sleeping over at Julie's.

I don't remember getting back to Riley's place, just the vague sensation that it was taking too long, that maybe we were lost. And I remember checking my phone over and over again, expecting my Mom to be furious. But all she sent was a single text:

Okay. Have fun. I need the car by 11 tho, for pottery class, k?

My next real moment of focus was when Riley

was tugging at my pants in his bedroom. I was shoving him back, saying "Wait . . . wait . . ."

"Then why the hell did you take the Viagra?!" he barked.

I winced at his voice and mumbled, "I didn't know that meant . . ."

"Why does *anybody* take a Viagra, Will?"

"I'm sorry . . . I . . ."

"Just forget it." And he slouched out of his clothes before falling like a chopped tree onto his mattress. The bedroom light was still on, making him seem like a corpse somehow. His pale skin visibly damp, his limbs bent at uncomfortable angles.

I left the room with the confused idea that I need-ed to add something to my stomach. I found myself out in Riley's living room, shivering in my under-wear, munching on saltine crackers. "Riley . . .?" I called into the bedroom. "Hey, Riley . . .?"

Something fell over and he shouted, "What?" But I didn't recognize the voice; it had gone hard and grey. I didn't respond. A moment later, I heard him mutter something and the bedroom light went out.

So I just stared out the window for a while, at the shadowy, snow-frosted towers all around. It was past the city's bedtime, and all the lights were out. But across the way there was a single lit window after all, where a boy was reading on his couch, alone. I wondered what kept him up. And wheth-er he wished he had company. Slowly, I realized every building down the street had at least one lit window. One out of every hundred windows was glowing with some person's mystery. I wondered if anyone was looking up at Riley's apartment. I wondered if I was somebody's nightlight. I sat up a long, long time, watching those far away lights. When I slept in brief patches, I was curled up on the sofa — wishing Riley would come out to rescue me, carry me back to bed. It didn't even matter that he was a bastard. Somehow all that mattered was the fact of his body. The fact of being alone versus the fact of being found.

Chapter 14

My next attack of sleep paralysis had a sense of drama — it arrived on Christmas morning. I was paralyzed for maybe two minutes. I could force my body to have a couple weak shudders, like I was being electrocuted, but otherwise I was really locked in.

Luckily, I was turned over and my face was stuffed in my pillow. So when I finally screamed myself awake, the sound was pretty muffled. I scrambled up, tore at the sheets and started rubbing my arms and legs to keep everything moving. Then I started stomping around my bedroom in my underwear chanting, "Ho Ho Ho! Ho Ho Ho!"

I could hear the coffee grinder growl downstairs. Mom and Dad would be making breakfast in their bathrobes. They put those stupid bathrobes on every year (the *good* bathrobes, you know?) like they were models for one of those cheap holiday cards they sell in drugstores.

But I couldn't take part in their fantasy. I pulled on jeans and a ratty old *Star Wars* T-shirt. I looked in the mirror that I'd hung on my closet door and said "Ho Ho Ho!" to the depressed-looking kid floating there.

In the kitchen, Dad was making Eggs Benedict from the old recipe he pulls down once a year. Mom was hovering behind him, offering nervous advice. When they spotted me, Dad called, "Hey, champ!" and Mom came over, chirping "Darling!" My dubious face stayed put while Mom gave me a big flannel hug. It was all fine, I guess. Only I wished it didn't feel like a show. Even people that love you are fakes.

When I was around fifteen, I realized the whole thing was a crock. We're all actors playing out Christmas movies for each other. Mom and Dad were pretending for me and I was pretending for them. Maybe it would have been different if I had brothers or sisters. But with just me, the whole thing was somehow really fragile. If anyone missed a step, it would collapse.

We had our Eggs Benny and coffee on the sofa and rooted through our stockings. Boxers. Chocolates. Lotto tickets. La-dee-da. I got some new science magazines, too.

Mom got weepy when I opened my biggest present — a new coat she'd driven into the city for. It was pretty great, actually. They call it a pea-coat, and it had big wooden buttons. When I wore it, I felt I was part of some classier time or part of a classier life. Mom was watching me wide-eyed. I could tell she'd be crushed if I didn't say how much I loved it. So I did.

Mom opened a scarf I'd bought for her at the Cottonwood Mall and Dad got a bocce ball set and then the whole thing was over. There we were, staring at each other wondering how to fill up the rest of the day. Dad asked if I wanted to play cards and I almost said yes because his face was so eager. But I just couldn't.

Mom had her dinner prep to keep her busy and Dad would be happier watching his reality television. So I told them I'd take my peacoat out for a test drive. Mom looked a little heartbroken. She started moving things around on the counter nervously, till she finally said, "God, Will, can't you even *try*? I'm trying here. Your Dad's trying here. Can't you just *try?*"

I winced. I never thought she'd say that out loud. That we were all *trying* to be a family. So I told her I guessed I couldn't try. That made her weepy. Only this time, it was for the worst reasons, and I couldn't fake my way out of it.

So I left. Not just for a walk around the block, either. I went walking through every stupid Chilliwack street, past all the houses where everyone I'd ever known was stuffing their face with chocolate or crashing on the couch while the TV sang them to sleep. I walked right around town. Past the Cottonwood Mall and the tiny park with its rusty swings. Straight through the movie theatre's empty parking lot. Until it was getting dark and I had to do up all the buttons on my brand new coat.

When I got back, dinner was already in the oven and it was smelling up the whole house. Mom and Dad were on the couch watching one of those black-and-white Christmas movies they play each year. *It's a Wonderful Life*. I sat and watched with them a while. That seemed to make my Mom happy, even though she wasn't exactly chatty.

We ate in front of the TV, too. Mom curled her legs up on the sofa and snuck under Dad's arm. They looked like a picture of a really happy couple, from my spot on the far side of the sofa. I had a memory-flash of being a little boy and crawling under my Dad's arm, or snuggling up with my Mom. Little kids are allowed those things. I tried to watch the TV, but being alone on that sofa was worse than being alone on Riley's.

I told them I wanted to read my new magazines in my room. I said goodnight and thanks for the coat.

"Do you really like it? Because we can take it back," said Mom. "They have lots of other kinds." She reached over the back of the couch and touched my arm. For a second I thought I might hug her.

"No, I like it. I really do."

She smiled up at me and then looked back to the TV.

Later, upstairs, I called Riley. I'd been tiptoe-ing around since that ugly night with the coke. But he'd asked me to call him on Christmas. He was spending the day with a few friends down-town. Orphans' Christmas, they called it; all their parents lived in other cities. When he answered the phone, I could hear a bunch of them shouting in the background. Some kind of drunken party game. My loneliness made me forgive.

"I miss you," I said. "Christmas is ridiculous."

"Aww," he chuckled into the phone. "This is only the practice version. Just you wait for Gay Christmas."

"When's that?"

"New Year's Eve, baby."

My mom appeared in the doorway, and I was surprised to see she had a drink in her hand. She'd washed off all her makeup too, and looked better for it, more natural. She saw I was on the phone, and put up her free hand to show she didn't expect me to stop my conversation. She just mouthed the words "Love you" and crept down the hall.

Chapter 15

Riley invited me to his apartment on New Year's Eve for "pre-drinks" before the big party at his friend's place down the block. We got pretty horny, drinking gin on his couch and talking about what we liked to do in bed. Of course, it was all made up on my part, but I was happy to use my imagination. And Riley, who knew I was making stuff up, kept saying, "Oh really? Oh *really*?"

When he went to take a leak, my phone started vibrating. I saw it was Daniel Federline. Call display told me I'd missed three calls from him that night. "Hello?"

"Oh. Hi, Will. How's it going?"

"Um, kinda busy, actually. Did you want something?"

"I was really just calling to chat. Can you . . . Can you talk for a sec?"

"Not really."

"It's just been sort of tough the past couple of weeks, I guess." He sounded really strangled, his voice all tight and scratchy. I knew that Adam and the other guys at school had been giving Daniel an especially hard time after he decided to show up wearing a blouse before Christmas break. I mean, really.

"I'm over at Riley's, actually," I said. "Shouldn't you be at a New Year's party or something?"

"You know, I just got so many invitations. In the end, I decided to stay home and watch *Ugly Betty* reruns with my parents."

"Ah."

And then, Jesus, I could hear him start to choke up on the phone. He was blubbering, and I really didn't know how to deal with that. "Come on," I said. "It's not like you'd even want to go to any of those stupid parties."

"Oh, God, Will, I'm not upset about the parties. It's not about some shitty parties!"

Riley was back from the bathroom and making us another drink in the kitchen. I could hear him laughing about something to himself and clinking the glasses around. "I've really got to go," I said.

"Did you know they shoved my face in Adam Becker's ass?"

"What?" I was shocked. But also sort of jealous.

"Not his *naked* butt. A bunch of them at lunch grabbed me in the parking lot. I was eating my lunch there alone because you and Julie were both off I-don't-know-where . . ."

"Oh, this is *my* fault?"

"I didn't *say* that!" He was getting hysterical. "They grabbed me and they said, 'Hey, faggot, you like ass. Have some ass.' And then Adam turned around and they started rubbing my face into the back of his jeans. I mean *hard*. And my lip got cut. I was bleeding and they just started laughing. It was . . . it was like . . ." But then Daniel started breathing hard, his voice veering in and out of control.

But there was nothing I could do about it then. I told him we'd talk about it the next day.

"Yeah. Fine."

"It's awful, though, Daniel. I'm sorry about all that."

"Whatever."

When I hung up, Riley handed me another gin and tonic. But I didn't feel like drinking anymore. I didn't even feel like going to the party. I saw Daniel's name on my phone, heard his choked-up voice in my head, and told myself *Don't get all delicate now. Don't be like that.* The stiff drinks were making my head sort of swim and I wanted to steady myself on something, someone. To be sure of something.

I'm not sure what got into me, but I said, "I don't need Viagra, you know."

Riley could really take a hint.

I'd seen him naked lots of times in the change room at the pool, but there's something quite different about seeing a guy naked in private. His skin felt warm, too warm, and it made me want to pause and just run my hands over his body. But he was impatient. He kept moving my arms around so I couldn't pay attention to anything. To be honest, all I wanted to do was rest on his chest. I kept trying to snuggle into his torso or lay my head on his arm and talk. But one thing led to another. And it's hard to stop that blur of limbs and lips once you start.

So, yeah, it happened. We did it. He used a condom and everything. I sort of went into a daze, like maybe this was just a porn video I was watching and not something that was actually happening to me. From beneath, his body seemed harder, heavier, and his dick kept jabbing angrily at my balls. He asked if he could put it inside me, and I thought that was funny. Like a gentleman asking if he could take my coat. He went slow, and I breathed deep, but it still hurt like hell. I tried not to wince, tried to make it look like I was twisting up my face from pleasure instead of shock.

He was saying, "You're doing great, buddy, you're doing so good." And I kept thinking how weird it was that he called me "buddy."

I know I was supposed to feel some profound connection. I know this was supposed to be a breakthrough of some kind. But all I felt was impatience for it to be over. His eyes were shut and his face was so serious — it almost seemed like an invasion of privacy to be watching him as he did it. When he came, I wanted badly to feel connected to what he was going through. I gripped at his waist, his flexing ass. But he was so, so far away. And he clenched his eyes tighter and tighter, the closer he got to finishing.

It was awkward as hell when he was finished. He backed out and tugged the full condom after himself. I was too nervous to look at it, for fear it'd be some horrible colour. But he tied a quick knot around the end and tossed the package into his garbage can like a pro.

And when it was all over, I could finally rest on his chest the way I'd wanted to from the start. He stroked my hair like I was just a kid and asked me if I was okay.

I kept saying, "Of course I'm okay." And he kept asking if I was sure, maybe because I'd gone all quiet. He talked about some stuff that didn't matter. About where we'd go for breakfast in the morning, and whether we should go to the New Year's Eve party at all. But I was hearing him say other things. I imagined him saying, "I'm going to take care of you," and "Why don't you move in with me?" and "You are so, so amazing."

Afterward . . . I had thought I would feel so connected. To him. To myself, even. But all I felt was that something had come undone, or something had failed to come together. It was the same damp feeling I had on the night we did cocaine with his friends. A brief spasm of hope, a pure sensation promising so much, followed by a long quiet stretch of fearful aloneness. I pressed myself tighter to his chest. But he said, "Babe, babe, I'm suffocating," and rolled away.

Chapter 16

In the morning, Riley brought me coffee in bed. He sat up against a stack of pillows reading out loud from the *Globe & Mail*. Something about a disaster. All I remember is the feeling of lying there next to him. I shuffled down so I could keep my head on his chest, against his ribs moving up and down as he read from the paper.

Then we went for a long swim and a quick steam. We got stared at a little by the Creep in his sad plastic sandals. He wasn't really that creepy at all, I decided. Just lonely.

Riley wanted to go for a walk by the water, but it turned out he wanted to have "a talk." I should have suspected it. People never want to go for a walk by the water just for the hell of it.

My brain took a little picture of him that morning in case he was about to break up with me. He looked good and scruffy. He hadn't shaved and the woolly old sweater he had on was something he'd picked up off his bedroom floor. Looking over at him, I wondered how many years a guy has when he can just roll out of bed and be that beautiful. How many years are there between the last pimple and the first wrinkle? Riley seemed to be right in the middle of that stretch of automatic handsome. When he started talking, though, his voice was tight. It reminded me of Daniel Federline's from the night before.

"Listen, Will, I have to tell you something. And I don't want you to freak out, okay?"

"That's a pretty bad start," I smiled, but Riley wasn't listening. He just kept staring ahead while he spoke and talked with a clear, loud voice like it was a long-distance call.

"Before we do anything like last night again, you should probably know that I'm HIV-positive."

That pulled a plug in my head. Things went dim and it was impossible to think or understand. After twenty seconds of silent furious walking, I managed to say, "You're telling me this *now*?"

"Don't worry. It's not like you're at any risk. I'm on meds, so my viral count is . . ."

But I couldn't hear any of it. I said again, "You're telling me this *now*?" He started talking about "antiretroviral drugs" and "viral loads." All I could think was *What did I do? What did I do?* There had been a condom, but not for everything.

Finally, I guess something in me switched on. I started shouting. "What are you *talking* about?

Why didn't you tell me before? Why didn't you tell me *before?!*"

"I didn't want you to freak out about it . . ." Riley looked exhausted. He wasn't meeting my gaze and kept scanning the ocean like he'd lost something there.

I didn't know what to say, so I started walking away as fast as I could manage without breaking into a run. Riley called out my name in a hassled way, like it was all a chore for him. That only made me madder.

If I had been a really noble, lovable guy, I might have stayed and talked it out. But I'm not that guy. When big things happen in real life, nobody ever says the right thing. In fact, I usually say the thing that does the most damage. The indelible thing. So the best I could do was leave before I said it.

I kept going until I got to the car, which had a ticket stuck to the windshield because I'd left it there overnight. I drove right out of town with the ticket flapping crazily under the windshield wiper. I finally lost it somewhere on the highway.

When I pulled into the driveway, my mom heard the car. She opened the front door before I got there. "Well," she said, "home at last." When I looked at her, though, her face just crumpled. "Baby," she said. "What in the world happened?"

***

Once I was safe in my room upstairs, I wanted badly to cry about it all. I wanted to call up Riley and yell at him, or throw my computer out the window. But all I could manage was stillness. I almost phoned Julie, but knew I'd just get shit after ignoring her for so long. Almost called Daniel. But how could I, after hanging up on him and his problems?

I tried playing every sad love song on my laptop, but nothing worked. In the end, I just lay on the floor and started reading a story in one of my science magazines about the distance between things in space. I got thinking about that cold impossible void between one tiny rock and the next one, and finally that worked. I got a couple good tears from that.

Chapter 17

From: rileyjustrileynoreally@live.com
To: willjohnsonomg@gmail.com
Sent: Jan 4, 2012 at 2:23 a.m.
Subject: Hey

Hi Will,

So . . .

It's two in the morning and I've just spent the last hour looking for a picture of you online. But there are too many Will Johnsons in the world so now I'm giving up. I even went back to Man-Tracker, to look at your profile page. But your page doesn't exist anymore. You deleted it?

Anyway, I know you might not even read this. I know you're pissed. But you won't return my calls and I've got to have a chance to explain. So you're getting a letter like in that old book you were going on about. (Something about prejudice?)

First things first: you're safe. What you didn't let me explain that day on the seawall is there's basically no way you could get HIV from me. When a guy's on his meds (and I am) the virus gets beaten back enough that just a bit of it floats around in your brain or something. Do some research if you want. You don't have to trust me.

I wish you could trust me, though. I know you feel betrayed or whatever but look at my position. Can you guess how many people go running if you tell them you're positive on the first date? It's like being a leper. Even my oh-so-Catholic mom freaked. The day after I told her, I caught her throwing out the cutlery I'd been using. People freak and they turn into assholes. You were sort of an asshole about it, actually. You didn't have to bolt like that. I spent the rest of the day wandering around the park and telling myself I wouldn't talk to you again.

So much for that.

I texted you, I called you. I even thought about coming out to Chilliwack and banging on your front door, but I don't know your address. That whole world of yours is a total mystery. And now I can't even stalk you right.

But I do wish you'd give me a chance. I miss having you around. I miss just listening to you geek out, and watching old Buffy episodes on the couch. I miss how you smell — did you know you smell like a (sexy) grandpa? All that Old Spice.

I'll sign off now. And don't worry, I'm not

going to start harassing you with soppy emails. If you want to be in touch, you know how. Ball's in your court.

And I'm sorry. I meant to say that in here some-where.

xo R

Chapter 18

Here's a handy thing about being a sullen jerk:
When you've actually got something to hide, your
parents can't tell the difference. For a week or so,
I'd come home and dodge Mom's nervous eyes,
just hike the stairs to my bedroom.

And then, one grey afternoon, I came home to
find my mom slouched on the staircase, a load
of laundry spilled on the steps beneath her. She
looked like she'd been sitting there a long, long
while.

"What's going on?" I climbed a couple steps
and sat beneath her.

"Don't get angry," she started.

"Why?"

"I was worried, and . . ." She was spinning
one hand in the air beside her head to pull out
her reasons. "I was worried. So I looked on
your computer."

"Mom!"

"I just wanted to know what was going on with you. You drive into town for this club of yours, but you never come back when you say you will. You never tell us if you're dating anyone. You never talk to us at all."

I half-listened while I made a furious inventory of recent web pages I'd visited. And the post-shower jerk-off session I'd had that morning . . . "That's my personal —"

"It *is* my business, Will. If there's something wrong. I just . . ." Her eyes were puffy. She started folding socks and lobbing them in the basket. "I need you to tell me if there's something wrong. I saw those websites."

I stared at the ceiling. "Everybody looks at porn, Mom."

She blinked at me and shook her head a little. "Oh, God, I don't care about porn. Your dad looks at porn, Will." She was examining a faded T-shirt of mine. "*I* look at porn. You know, sometimes you act like you're the only person in this house with a life. I'm talking about the AIDS stuff. All these web pages about living with AIDS."

"Oh. Oh, *that*! That's research."

She fixed me with a look. And then there were thirty full seconds of silence while Mom just watched me. I looked at the laundry, at my hands, at the peeling paint on the ceiling. When my eyes warily came back to her face, she was still staring. Everything ridiculous about her — all the weak nervous laughter and timid questions that made up the bulk of our life together — had washed away. Instead, there was something cutthroat and sure underneath. "I can wait all day," she said.

So I told her. About Riley, about us having sex and him being HIV-positive. Mom was relieved for a nanosecond that it wasn't me who was positive, and then her anxiety swung to "that boy."

At dinner, Mom brought Dad up to speed. When I mentioned Riley was twenty-three, she said that was criminal, wasn't it? Whatever that thing was that we had on the steps, it had vanished. Things were crumbling.

"This is your life we're talking about," said Mom. "You cannot keep seeing this boy." She kept giving her head these little rough shakes like there was something stuck in her hair, her eyes.

"I wasn't really planning to," I told her.

"I should hope not," said Mom. "This is your *life!*" she said again. I'm not sure what that meant exactly.

But I was getting defensive by then, on Riley's behalf. I decided to try something out. I said, "Hold on. Wouldn't you want somebody to date me if *I* got some virus? Or would you want me to never have a boyfriend at all?"

They didn't have an answer for that, but Mom rolled her eyes like the question was ridiculous. "The point is, Will . . . The point is that you're not going to put yourself in a position where that could happen."

"But nobody *means* to put themselves in that position," I mumbled.

And then Dad really surprised me. He slammed his hands down on the kitchen table and shouted, "Don't be a jackass, Will! You think this is funny? Well I'll tell you, boy, you will *not* think this is funny if you get stuck with something that's going to wreck your life. Because that's what it does, I hope you know. It *wrecks* people's lives."

Riley's life didn't seem so wrecked to me. But I just said not to worry, that I wasn't planning on seeing him again. I looked at the table. "I'll be a monk until you both die, if that makes you more comfortable."

Dad looked wounded and weary. I didn't know I could do that to him. "Let's not be like this," he said.

"This is what we're like," I said.

"Not really. I don't think that."

I finished my dinner in silence and let Mom and Dad drift off into talk about work and the weather — anything to keep the real subject at bay.

That night, up in my room, I was still angry enough I couldn't read. I stared for hours at the ceiling, imagining the water stains were galaxies and nebulas whose light was just reaching the Earth after travelling through space for millions and millions of years.

My phone rang and I saw it was Julie. I guess I picked up as a reflex, but I really wasn't in the mood to talk to her. She said, "Listen, I have to tell you something."

"I've actually got my own stuff going on right now," I said.

"It's not as important as this."

That got me crazy mad. "How could you know?" I demanded. "How could you possibly know?" I hung up on her and threw the phone across the room. The black mark it left on the wall was the most satisfying thing I'd seen all day.

***

At breakfast the next morning, we were all trying to reboot. Dad was digging into his grapefruit with a tiny spoon and making a mess of it. Mom made me porridge. I sat like a good son and asked for the Sports section. Dad raised his eyebrows but passed it over. "By the way," he said, "I was talking to Adam Becker's dad at the office. Apparently they got an acceptance letter from the University of Toronto. Early admission, I think he said. That what they call it, Will?"

Mom, always the peacemaker, smiled at me. "You'll get yours. It's coming."

I looked at Dad while I chewed my toast. "Yup. Early acceptance. The letters are only starting to come, though. There's lots of time." I started imagining Adam Becker on a university hockey team. And that quickly led to the hockey team's change room, the showers . . .

"Is there still time to apply to more schools, by

the way? Seems a shame you put all your eggs in one basket."

Looking up from my plate, I felt sorry for Dad, trying way too late to guide me with that tiny spoon clutched in his hand. "The deadlines are all past," I told him.

He looked at me for a second, then gave me a tight-lipped smile and went back to the paper. "It'll all work out," he said to the news. "And, besides, you could always get your real estate licence."

Mom smiled at that and something came into focus for me: Neither of them had ever lived outside of Chilliwack, much less set foot on a university campus. They had a whole other future in mind. And, to them, it wasn't smaller or less valuable than the one I was dreaming of.

I was heading upstairs to shower when my phone started dancing in my pocket. Julie.

"Hey. Sorry about last night. But I honestly still can't talk."

"Okay, but give me one minute."

"Really? We can't go over whatever drama this is at school?"

"Will, you're such an ass. I've been trying to tell you that Daniel's in the hospital. He tried to kill himself."

Chapter 19

I skipped class that morning and biked to the hospital. I found Daniel in his room, deep in the building's labyrinth of halls. He was lying in bed like in a movie or something. Two old ladies were laid out at the far end of the room, sort of drooling on their pillows and watching *The Price is Right* with the TV on mute.

When I walked in, I looked really quick for bandages on Daniel's wrists. But I guess he'd done it with pills because his skin wasn't marked up at all. His face looked crazy-white, like he'd been throwing up, and I thought maybe they gave him something to make him puke it all out.

He said, "Hey," and I said, "Hey." We looked at each other for a long moment. I wasn't sure who was supposed to begin, so I pulled a chair up and sat beside his bed. I put my feet on the edge of his mattress.

"So how goes, Mr. Federline?" I was going for casual. "How do you feel?"

"The same," he said. And that shut me up pretty fast. We watched the silent TV for a bit, because some guy had won a car and people were doing wild, happy dances on the screen.

The weird thing about visiting people in the hospital is that it's boring. They can't move around and you can't talk about your own problems, so conversation is limited. The robot bed is only amusing for a couple minutes, tops.

We talked about nothing for a while. Then, when Daniel went silent again, I blurted out, "So why'd you do it, Daniel? It's so . . . stupid."

And he looked up at the TV in this really re-laxed way, like he was counting to ten. Then he said, matter-of-factly, "I was just too tired. I woke up two days ago and something had fallen over inside me overnight. I couldn't conceive of having a shower, let alone leaving the house or talking to people." He was working at folding the edge of his bedsheets just so. "Now they have me under observation, they say, which means a nurse looks in at me every half-hour and makes sure I'm not trying to hang myself."

I nodded, bit my lip, and rubbed my hands on the top of my legs like I was waiting for something to happen. One of the old ladies peered our way from her bed and fixed her drooping eyes on whatever she saw in us. Daniel just lay there, ready for me to say something, but I didn't know what. He looked like a mini version of those broken-down soldiers you see in war movies, a tight, white sheet pinning him down to the sagging mattress. There must have been something I could have said, something to show him I was on his side after all. But I felt awful, and the room was too small, and the smell of sanitization was everywhere. I couldn't stand to be there anymore, and it made me feel reckless. I said, "You're not going to try it again, are you?"

"No, I don't think so." Daniel looked like the idea made him sleepy. Had they drugged him? "It sort of . . . took something out of me when I . . . It's not that I feel any different — not at all. But all this . . ." He waved his arm around the hospital room. "All this isn't a good fix, I guess."

"Hm." I stood up to show I had to get going and Daniel surprised me by picking up my hand. He sort of shook it and squeezed it, in an awkward but hopeful way. My eyes started to burn, and I worried they would leak. So I gave him a quick smile and made up an excuse to get the hell out of there.

Chapter 20

After scarfing down a packaged sandwich in the hospital cafeteria, I biked across town to Spencer High. I figured I should at least make an appearance at my afternoon classes. As I cut across the Cottonwood Mall parking lot, a few moms looked up at me from their rattling shopping carts with the dozy eyes of cattle.

Julie had texted me three question marks (**???**) because I was missing the start of English lit. When I finally appeared and collapsed in a pile beside her, she raised her eyebrows at me like she was mentally texting me some more. "How nice of you to join us," jabbed Mrs. Buchanon.

I couldn't concentrate, of course, on the nineteenth-century novel we were reading. Now the tea parties, the polite disagreements, the anxieties about marrying wealthy men seemed inane. But Mrs. Buchanon droned on, her mound of mousy hair pierced with a Bic but still wobbling in its pile atop her head.

While some poor girl in the front row got grilled, Laura Kwan turned around in her seat and fixed Julie with her School President smile. She whispered, "Hey, Jules, Adam's parents went to Tofino for the weekend so we're having a house party tonight. You should totally come. It's gonna be, like, massive."

Julie, who couldn't stand being called "Jules," shot me a quick look. She said, "Totally. Can I bring Will?"

Even Laura couldn't get out of inviting me when I was sitting right there. She smiled as though only noticing me at that moment. "Totally," she said. Then her smile clicked down into a serious face and she instructed us both, "Bring booze."

After class, Laura caught up with me in the hall. She took hold of my elbow and began walking with me arm-in-arm, *Pride and Prejudice*–style. It made me think of poor Daniel, back in the hospital. I saw the looks of surprise that kids in the hall were shooting us and hated myself for the hit of pride I felt. "Listen, Will," said Laura. "About the party tonight."

"I don't have to come if you don't want me there."

"Not *want* you there!" She placed a hand on her heart and opened her mouth into an O to show her shock. "Of *course* you're invited, Will. For sure.

I just wanted to have a *quick* chat with you about Adam's family. Just so you understand. You know they're, like, *super* Christian, right?"

"Yeah, I got that impression."

"So I just don't think it'd make for a comfortable atmosphere if things got all. . . political, you know? So, like, just don't bring a boyfriend or whatever."

I wasn't sure how to respond.

"It's not like I'm prejudiced. I am *so* not prejudiced," she went on. "It's just that there's a time and place, right?"

I heard myself say, "Totally," as though I were talking while driving. Once she got that out of me, she dropped my arm.

"I knew you'd understand," she smiled. With that, Laura Kwan kissed my cheek — she *kissed* my goddamn cheek — and went gliding down another hall.

"What the hell was that?" Julie had come up behind me and was staring after Laura.

"I think I was just put back in the closet."

Julie looked at me in a hard sort of way. I could tell she was still annoyed with the way I'd been acting, but she hated small-town bigots much more. "Time to burn the closet down," she said. "See you tonight? You're not busy with Riley?"

I gave her a smile to warn her off pursuing the issue. "We're not so much."

"Oh." She looked down the hall, as if trying to calculate something. "Sorry about that."

"No, you're not."

"Well, I wish I was sorry."

"That's something."

***

After school, Julie and I stole a couple six-packs from her dad's garage stash and drank a few in the alley behind the Safeway. We talked about Daniel some, about Julie's dad some. But mostly we talked about nothing, the way we had done for years. It felt good to just waste time with her and make snarky remarks about the adults in our lives. Julie crushed an empty can beneath her boot and said, "I've been trying to figure out how it begins, how people transform into the dull bowls of porridge they all end up as."

"Oh, yeah?" I was smirking but interested.

"Yeah. And I got it figured out. It's the weather."

"All right, I'll bite. What about the weather?"

"Well," she cracked a new can. "It's actually the weather *report*. There's a moment in a person's early thirties when they start talking about the weather *report* — not just about the fact its raining right now but what the weather is going to be like, what the weather was like last year. Et cetera. Et cetera."

"And that's some kind of trap?"

"It's the beginning of dull. Weather is a gateway drug to dull. After people start talking about the weather they think it's okay to talk about their

121

mortgages. And then, hey, if we're talking about mortgages we might as well talk about the price of gas. From there you can give up and spend your life discussing your kid's bowel movements . . ." She trailed off like the line of thought was continuing, silently, in her head. Then she lobbed an empty can into the bushes. "Hey, Will?"

"Yeah?"

"Let's never talk about the weather. Promise me that, okay?"

I stopped fiddling with the metal tab on my can and looked at her. The sight of her shaved head in the last few rays of sunlight made me suddenly, unaccountably, happy. "Let's get this over with," I said. And she understood. We headed together in the direction of Adam's house. That empty can of hers is probably still there, rusty and buried, crumpled by Julie's anxious hands.

***

You could hear the party down the block — it sounded like a hockey riot. Julie and I were already half-drunk and rolling our eyes at each other as we climbed the front steps — the only possible response to the horrible blur of girlie screams and macho hooting inside. The door had been propped open with a moss-covered gnome so we let ourselves through. I dropped my new coat on the pile in the hall. Julie handed me another beer from her backpack. "Into the fray, Mr. Johnson." She placed a hand on my shoulder and started guiding me toward the backyard, where most of the kids had collected.

Laura Kwan was playing the perky host and came to greet us right away. She'd done up her face with some kind of glitter makeup, which made her look like a twelve-year-old ready for her princess-themed birthday. "Omigod, you *made* it!" she cheered. Then she gave Julie a hug while balancing a couple plastic cups of cider in her hands. "Aw!" she said, stepping back and looking at Julie's outfit. She was acting like we were visiting from another country — which, in a way, we were.

"Well, make yourselves at home, guys. I just gotta . . ." She raised the two plastic cups up by way of explanation and nudged past us.

Out back, nearly naked kids were cannonballing into Adam's heated pool and shivering on the lawn, laughing at each other over the rims of their drinks. It didn't take long for Julie to start getting looked at. Whenever she deigned to appear at parties, guys always went for her. I was ready to play wingman when Nicholas Humphries went sauntering by. But Julie gave me an eyebrow wiggle and asked, instead, if she could fly solo.

"You'll be all right?" she asked.

"Oh, I'm fine," I said. And I gave her a little shove in Nicholas's direction.

Suddenly stranded in the crowd, I looked around. I was standing maybe three metres from Adam and his pack. And when I focused in, I found they were sniggering about Daniel. I could catch little snatches of their conversation beneath the music: "Such a pussy" . . . "Better luck next time, eh?" . . . "He totally did it to get attention" . . . "Maybe I should send him a picture of my dick to cheer him up."

That last one was Adam. He grabbed at his crotch as he said it, and the guys around him started laughing like a bunch of hyenas. And then something in me snapped. Maybe it was the beers and maybe it was the horrible shouting of all those manic teenagers. But I stared at the back of Adam's crewcut head and started shaking like part of me had come loose.

Beneath those bleary party lights in Adam's backyard, it all became obvious: I needed to take a stand, just like in the movies. Not because it was the right thing to do, but because I'd never be able to live with myself if I didn't. All the measly, bigoted comments that Adam and his friends had been hurling at Daniel for years were now being hurled at me, too. I'd never realized how angry I was. And I'd never been so clear on what I should do about it. I was wobble-legged from beer, but I was sure.

"Hey!" I shouted. "Hey, Adam!"

His head craned toward me, still contorted by the laughter at his own joke. The semicircle of guys around him looked at me, too. Their faces were lit with the anticipation of something going down.

"Something wrong, Mr. Johnson?" Adam took

a sip of his beer and cocked his head to one side.

I took a step toward them. My voice crumpled a little as I continued. "Daniel's in the hospital *because* of you, you know that? You do understand that it's your fault, right?"

Adam dumped the remainder of his beer on the grass and let his cup fall to the ground. He took a step forward and squinted at me. "What are you, his boyfriend?"

"They're totally bum buddies," laughed one of the guys behind him. "Totally!"

I took a swing. This was not the brightest decision, I suppose, given Adam's size, his hockey career, his four snarling pals behind him. But it felt pretty great to get one sucker punch in, to see Adam's stunned eyes in the moment my fist made contact with his perfect square jaw. There was a second, maybe two, of silence, as Adam's face turned back toward me. His lip had split and a trickle of blood bloomed there, wet and bright.

And then he was on me — slamming my body backward onto the lawn and pinning my arms down with his knees. He used one hand to grip my neck, taking aim. And then it came, blow after blow across my face. For some reason I kept shouting, "Hey! Wait! Hey!" Like there was some mistake. But no. This was exactly what was meant to happen.

Before long the other boys were dragging Adam off me, with a chorus of "Dude! Dude!" Like even they felt enough was enough. A few kids were staring at us, but nobody moved. As Adam stood over me, a boot on either side of my torso, a nearby party lantern was swinging in the wind so his features were lost in darkness, then illuminated, then lost again. There was a glimmer of something liquid. I thought maybe his bloody lip was dripping. But then he spit a gob of saliva from his puckered mouth. It was cold when it hit my face. Later I would remember this as an almost erotic moment. His heaving body standing above me. The feel of his spit on my face. But at the time, there was only stupid, childish terror. My bit of bravery was spent, and now I only wanted to escape.

"Get out of here," said Adam. He nudged my ribs with his toe.

I got myself onto hands and knees and then, wincing, stood up and shuffled back toward the house. I could hear him say, "Faggot," to his friends, as though it were a one-word explanation. But nobody laughed. The yard had gone silent by then. One or two kids muttered, "Not cool, man." But nobody really stood up for me. Why would they? Until that night, I'd never stood up for anything or anyone.

Where was Julie? Upstairs, making out with Nicholas, I figured. Let her enjoy it. I tried to rescue my new coat from the pile by the door. But I couldn't find it. It was stolen, or lost among the others. So, shivering, I made my way down the street. I said to myself: *That's what I thought. That's what I thought.*

Chapter 21

The next morning, my mangled face did a number on Mom and Dad. They knew without me telling them that it was somehow part of "the gay thing." Mom made waffles while Dad sat me down at the kitchen table and got it out of me. I refused to name names. A phone call to Adam's parents wouldn't fix anything.

"Oh, Will!" said my mom. "You need to be safe about these things. Here, use the good syrup. If you're going to — if you're going to *advertise* yourself, then people are going to react."

Even as she was saying it, I saw she realized the subtext of her words: *Don't be so obvious, Will. Don't be gay for real.* She piled another waffle on my plate to make up for it. And that gave me an excuse to say, "Thanks, Mom."

Once Dad realized what had happened, he came around the kitchen table and crushed me into the side of his baggy suit in a lock of a hug. "We love you, guy." I let him hold on as long as he liked, listing sideways in my chair, wondering why it was only violence and shock that could make him say these things out loud.

***

I kept my head pretty low after that.

Daniel came back to school a week later. The three of us returned to our lunch routine, our circular patterns of chatter and gossip. Only we were gentler with each other now. I told them about Riley and they nodded silently, finally beyond wisecracks. Daniel brought up my fight with Adam just once, by reaching out to touch my swollen lip and solemnly saying, "Ouch." It felt like a blessing.

Once my face had healed some, I started swimming my laps every day after school again. One, two, breathe. One, two, breathe. Before I knew it, a couple months had gone by and it was almost the end of the school year.

At long last, a letter from UBC came in the mail. I opened it alone in my bedroom and read it through twice before returning it to its envelope. Then I waited until dinner to show it to Mom and Dad. I wanted their full attention.

My dad looked at the letter as though he couldn't be expected to understand the language. Then he put down his wine and waved it in the air. "So. Is this *late acceptance*, then? Is that what they call it?"

"Yeah, Dad. Late acceptance." He had knocked the wind out of the thing, but I saw that he didn't know what he was doing. Mom's congratulations, too, were dim and underwhelming. Or was there, beneath that, a kind of envy?

Either way, it didn't matter that they were missing the greatness of it. I was happy on my own, and that wasn't changing. My grades were going to squeak me into a future. I had just barely won myself a shot. I took my letter upstairs and actually kissed it before tucking it into my bedside drawer. It was the best letter I'd ever got. I hadn't admitted to myself how much I cared until it arrived.

After dinner, I went for my swim at the Chilliwack rec centre. Something about the idea of "my future" made me want to just go and go, until I got so tired I was sucking in mouthfuls of water. Then I sat a while on the edge of the pool and watched the other swimmers moving in their own little lanes, their own little worlds. One, two, breathe. One, two, breathe. If you go swimming enough, you get so the smell of chlorine actually calms you down. I love that chemical smell. I love the echoes of people shouting. And the old women doing their meaningless water aerobics. And the couples playing footsie beneath the Jacuzzi's bubbles.

In the change room, I was drying off in front of a mirror when, mindlessly, I dropped the towel to my side and just looked at my body. There was something surprising about it. My chest looked larger in the mirror than I remembered it. My arms were bigger, too. In fact, my whole torso made a great sort of triangle, spreading from my waist out to my shoulders. I looked like the men I used to stare at in underwear ads. And it sort of stunned me. I sort of wanted to feel myself.

The only thing that shook my gaze off the mirror was the ropey guy in basketball gear who went walking by just then. He was looking at me the way I'd been looking in the mirror. I smiled, but he flinched like I'd thrown something at him.

Chapter 22

"That's it?"

"That's it."

"It's so tiny. It's almost cute."

"Size can be deceiving. This is one nasty bugger."

Daniel flipped the microscopic crab off his finger and squashed it on the sidewalk.

"How long till you're itch-free?"

"I have to be lathered all day in this neurotoxin I got at the pharmacy. Plus I had to, you know, *shave*."

"Oh, gross."

"The price of love, Will."

"Who *gave* you crabs in the first place?" We traded Slurpies and kept on walking.

Daniel weighed his head back and forth as he sucked on his straw. "After my little *episode* in the hospital, I decided to start living a bit more. So I finally responded to one of those guys online."

"You're shitting me."

"You know the guy at the Chevron?"

I gave him a shoulder hit. "The *old* guy??"

"Ow! And yes. He was nice. For what I wanted, anyway."

"Mr. Federline, I am royally impressed."

"Well, I'm not altogether sure it was worth the price." I could see him itching at his crotch through his pocket. "But speaking of consequences, you *did* get yourself tested, didn't you?"

We turned toward the park and headed for the rusty swings. "Not yet, no. It's not like there was any real risk. It'd just be to make myself feel better."

"We don't just do these things for ourselves, though." Daniel pumped his chest forward and back, gaining more height on each swing. "You do it for your friends' peace of mind, too. And you do it so you can tell whoever you bonk next that you've been tested."

I swung in silence a while, looking out at the abandoned playground. It was well into March, and daffodils were trumpeting around the edges of things. "I know," I said. "I know . . ."

"There's a place on Davie Street, you know, where you can go and get tested for HIV while you wait. Fast-food health care."

And so, months after the horrible morning when I'd last seen Riley, I took myself into town. I sat in a tiny room, rolled up my sleeve, and looked the other way while a nurse stuck a needle in. Then we chatted a bit while we waited for the

132

results. He told me it was good to come in as a precaution, but that the chances of my catching anything were almost zero. He started explaining about viral loads, like Riley tried to, only this time I could hear. The pills kill enough of the virus, he said, so it can't really spread anymore. "You're safer having sex with a positive guy who's on his meds then you are just picking someone up at the bar," said the nurse.

Then it was time to look at the results. I could feel my heart against my ribs. I wondered if I was going to lose it. When the nurse dryly said, "Negative," I blanked on what that meant.

"Negative is good," he smiled. "Negative means no virus."

I walked out into the afternoon, more relieved than was sensible. Then, in a rush, I was thinking about Riley, how I'd disappeared and never returned his calls. I wish I was the sort of person who's always kind. But I just can't do it when I'm scared.

I walked until I found this little park where people were playing with their dogs and smoking in the grass. I lay down there and stared up at the sky for a while. If I stare long enough, I think I can see the curve of the atmosphere as easily as my bedroom ceiling. While I lay there, I thought about the end of high school. How small it would one day seem compared to the business of living a life in the impossibly huge world.

My reverie was broken by the vibrations of my phone: Julie.

133

Guess who's downtown for once? (Grad dress shopping :()

In that moment there was nobody else I wanted to see. Visiting the clinic had somehow made me feel less grown-up, not more. I texted her my co-ordinates, and only ten minutes later I glimpsed her shaved head on the far side of the park. She was carrying something. As she got closer, I realized it was my peacoat, the one I'd lost at Adam's party. "Well, hello, stranger," she said.

"Where the hell did you find that?"

She handed over the coat and gave me a friendly smile. "Ran into one of Adam's crowd wearing it yesterday. He denied that he'd stolen it at first. But I started making a scene in the middle of Cotton-wood Mall. Nothing like the stares of twenty bored shoppers to get a guy doing the right thing."

"You're amazing." I pulled the jacket on and ran my hand over its buttons. "You didn't have to go and make a stand for me."

"Well, you stood up for Daniel."

"Did I?" It had felt, at the time, like I was standing up for myself. Maybe there wasn't much difference.

As I buttoned up my coat, I started saying, "Well. Well . . ." And then my breath got ragged, and I had to scrub my hands across my face to stay together. "By the way," I said finally, "I'm sorry I disappeared this year."

"You did and you didn't," Julie said.

Chapter 23

Our graduation ceremony was, of course, a bit of a joke. I would have skipped it entirely, but my parents were really into it. Mom bought a new dress from Winners and everything. We shuffled across the gym floor while the school band lurched through "Pomp and Circumstance." Real classy.

Julie and I were a team again. We sat together, and Daniel sat with us, too. The game, naturally, was to make little comments about all the jerks when they went to get their diplomas. Adam Becker looked like a total ape when he got up there, and he gave the principal this huge dramatic handshake like he was meeting the President of the United States. What a moron. I gave a *whoot* for Julie when she went up and we both gave a *whoot* for Daniel. Actually, quite a few people did, which seemed to surprise him. When I walked across the stage, I could hear my mom shout, "All right,

Will!" like she was watching a hockey game. It might have been embarrassing, but I didn't mind.

Will Johnson is in the first half of the alphabet, so I had a stretch of time to relax in the third row of folding chairs and watch everyone else. I watched the Lees and the Nelsons and the Richardsons and the Smiths all stride across the risers to shake that bored principal's hand. Sometimes I thought it looked lame, and sometimes I felt as proud as the parents behind us. I felt like those kids had done something, or been somewhere, though I couldn't say what or where.

I thought about all the millions of things I didn't know about those kids. I made silent bets with myself on who would get pregnant in the back of a car. And who would drink their life away. And who would spend their days, happier, far happier than me, bagging groceries at the Safeway. But I guess you never know. I figure there were two or three hundred of us in that big, broken auditorium, and every last one of us was living on a separate planet.

***

Afterward, a few of us went out for burgers at the Dairy Queen. While we were waiting for our dinners to come, Daniel told a story about how he'd almost joined the Hari Krishna group down at the mall. "How was I to know they believe in love and peace for everybody except homos?"

I smiled at him and Julie laughed root beer out her nose. "Gimme a sec, guys," I said. And I stepped out to the parking lot to call Riley. It was the first hot day of the year. When I sat on the curb, I could feel heat radiating off a line of gleaming cars.

It'd been months since we'd spoken, but Riley picked up like he was expecting my call. A big, happy, "Hey, *you*!" And he launched into telling me about his promotion at the real estate agency. When I told him today was my grad, he sort of laughed — still amused by the mention of high school, my other world he never had access to.

"Did you get into any universities, by the way?"

"Yeah, I'm going to UBC." Through the DQ window, I could see the animated faces of my friends. I was missing more stories. "My friend Julie's going to the college out here. And Daniel got a goddamn scholarship to McGill."

Riley laughed at my excitement for people he didn't know. "Well, nice! Good for you." He seemed honestly happy, like it wasn't his manners talking or anything. "You know, me and some of the guys are going out near UBC next weekend. We're doing a bonfire down at Wreck Beach. You should come."

I said, "Sure."

Chapter 24

"You didn't tell Will that Wreck is a nudie beach?" Matt, the one who reminded me of Daniel Federline, was laughing in short guffaws as we made our way down the trail toward the water. Riley looked over his shoulder at me and shrugged.

"Exactly *how* nudie is it?" I asked.

Matt told me that on a hot August weekend it was the most naked place on Earth. But right then, given that it was just the start of spring, he figured we'd be the only people down there.

"Unless you want to venture into the Pop-Up Forest," said someone behind me.

Riley waited for me to catch up and put an arm around my shoulder. He pointed through the woods while we went down, down, down the never-ending dirt path. "The Pop-Up Forest is where guys go for sex out here." I gave Riley a look and he said, "You don't need to worry. It's all very orderly. If you don't go past this one set of logs, no one will even approach you."

When we finally hit the sand, the sun was already setting, playing orange and gold on the waves. It felt a million miles from the city. It was beautiful, I had to admit. The guys started tugging off their shirts and shorts and even their underwear. Before long, I was the weird one wearing clothes. Staying dressed was only going to make everyone stare, so I sat on a log and started fiddling with my shoes.

"Atta boy!" cheered Matt, and I rolled my eyes. Actually, once I was naked it didn't take long before it felt normal. There's not much to be shocked about once you get over yourself. All our dicks, in fact, just looked funny and shrivelled from the cool air. There wasn't much sexy about it. But the breeze felt amazing, I can tell you.

Some of the guys started collecting wood for a fire, and Matt tugged a couple old quilts from his bag. Our clothes could have kept us warm, but once you've got that salt air on your body, the idea of getting dressed sounds like scrubbing yourself with sandpaper.

Riley suggested we go for a swim before it got too dark, so we ducked into the waves together. We hooted at the cold and swam straight out into the ocean. We swam for a solid five minutes, until it got almost scary how far away the land was. Especially as the light was failing.

Still, we felt alive out there on the water at night. There were hardly any waves, so Riley and I could float on our backs. There was something about hovering there in the dark that really calmed me down — floating, bobbing, being held.

"You know," I said quietly, "this doesn't mean we're getting back together."

"I know that." His voice sounded disembodied at first. But then I felt around with my foot and locked legs with him, to make a raft of our bodies.

"It's not because you're positive," I said.

"It sort of is," came his voice.

I let a lungful of air slip slowly over my lips and decided to be honest, honest, honest. "It's partly about that," I said. "It's also that I want to be . . . more connected. I want to feel like I'm on the same team as the other guy."

"And that didn't happen with us?"

"Not for me. I was feeling like a bit of a project for you, I guess. Or a . . . a toy."

"Aw!" Riley splashed me. "Not a toy. I just wasn't putting the relationship bar as high as you were." His foot rubbed the length of my calf in a thoughtful way, and part of me wanted badly to reach for him. "The older you get, the less you expect a cosmic connection."

I didn't have anything to say about that. But I silently promised myself I wouldn't stop hoping. Then Riley said the water was too cold, and he started swimming back to the beach. Before long, I could hear him laughing with the other guys, but sounds were really soft coming over the water. I wanted to stay out there as long as my body could stand the temperature. The stars were just starting to show. I thought about the speed of light — about the millions of years it took for the light from those stars to hit my eye that night on the ocean. I thought how strange it was to be lying there in one time and looking up at another time that was supposed to be over. It was like time was sort of sloshing around, the same as the ocean beneath me. Some of those stars could have already blown up, but there they were.

I don't want to sound like a poet, but a strange feeling came over me then. For one tiny moment, my brain stopped buzzing and my mouth cracked open. I was connected to everything. It felt like there was no difference between me and the water I was floating in. No difference between the time I was in and everything that came before me. No difference between me and the guys on the beach. That was the moment. Right then. I could see that it was possible to be myself and still be part of everything around me. It felt like an enormous relief.

It is possible to be apart from things and part of them at the same time. It is possible to be both separate and connected.

Then a thought came into my head: Were my limbs falling asleep? Was I going to have one of my attacks and not be able to wake my body? Would I drown in the black ocean, with all those guys laughing on the beach? Should I scream myself awake? My muscles jerked, and the water sloshed once, with a chop, around me.

But I didn't scream. And my limbs weren't dead after all. I was awake. I willed myself upright. I treaded water while running my hands over my legs, my chest, my face, to be sure of myself.

The ocean was freezing now, after all, so I started swimming as hard as I could. The guys had a fire going on the beach. As I swam, I could see the dark shapes of their bodies huddled around its light. It felt good, for once, to not be doing laps. It felt good to be swimming toward something real. Riley's shout — "There he is!" — set off some half-ironic applause as I walked, naked and shivering, onto dry land.

Moments later, I was under a blanket, looking into the fire while the others told a round of dirty jokes. I had an undeniable urge to connect with Julie. So I dug my phone out of my bag and texted her two words:

Miss you.

It shot up to space and down to her.

A minute later, a buzz came hurtling back from the stars:

Miss you, too. Gonna be home tomorrow?

For sure.

Author's Note

Will Johnson comes of age only when he finds a way to be both an individual and connected to the people around him. His struggle is — in some ways — typical. Too many gay, lesbian, and trans youths still feel divorced from society.

If you or your friends need a connection, check out the networks and resources for queer youth available online. You might want to start with: The Trevor Project (thetrevorproject.org), the Make it Better Project (makeitbetterproject.org), and It Gets Better (itgetsbetter.org).

We'd all be hopeless without our support teams. Mine includes three different families: a biological family (I lucked out and got a lovely one), a work family (cheers to the Dominion Writers Group and my pals at Transcon), and a friend family (my ideal readers).

Thanks, also, to the folk at Lorimer who so generously guided me through this project.